Angels at Moonglow

A Moonglow Christmas Novella

Deborah Garner

Cranberry Cove Press

Copyright © 2024 Deborah Garner

Cranberry Cove Press / Published by arrangement with the author

Angels at Moonglow by Deborah Garner

All rights reserved. Except for brief text quoted and appropriately cited in other works, no part of this book may be reproduced in any form, by photocopying or by electronic or mechanical means, including information-storage-or-retrieval systems, without permission in writing from the copyright owner/author.

This is a work of fiction. Names, characters, places and incidents either are products of the author's imagination or are used fictitiously. Any resemblance to actual events or locales or persons, living or dead, is entirely coincidental.

Cranberry Cove Press, PO Box 1671, Jackson, WY 83001, United States

Cover design by Mariah Sinclair | www.mariahsinclair.com

Library of Congress Catalog-in-Publication Data Available

Garner, Deborah

Angels at Moonglow / Deborah Garner—1st United States edition 1. Fiction 2. Woman Authors 3. Holidays

p. cm.

978-1-952140-29-7 (paperback)

978-1-952140-30-3 (hardback)

Printed in the United States of America 10 9 8 7 6 5 4 3 2

Angels at Moonglow

Books by Deborah Garner

The Paige MacKenzie Mystery Series

Above the Bridge
The Moonglow Café
Three Silver Doves
Hutchins Creek Cache
Crazy Fox Ranch
Sweet Sierra Gulch

The Moonglow Christmas Novella Series

Mistletoe at Moonglow
Silver Bells at Moonglow
Gingerbread at Moonglow
Nutcracker Sweets at Moonglow
Snowfall at Moonglow
Yuletide at Moonglow
Starlight at Moonglow
Joy at Moonglow
Evergreen Wishes at Moonglow
Angels at Moonglow

The Sadie Kramer Flair Series

A Flair for Chardonnay
A Flair for Drama
A Flair for Beignets
A Flair for Truffles
A Flair for Flip-Flops
A Flair for Goblins
A Flair for Shamrocks

Additional Titles

Cranberry Bluff
Sweet Treats
More Sweet Treats

Contents

Chapter 1	1
Chapter 2	7
Chapter 3	13
Chapter 4	19
Chapter 5	25
Chapter 6	31
Chapter 7	37
Chapter 8	43
Chapter 9	49
Chapter 10	55
Chapter 11	61
Chapter 12	67
Chapter 13	73
Chapter 14	79
Chapter 15	85
Chapter 16	91
Chapter 17	97
Chapter 18	103
Betty's Cookie Exchange Recipes	107
Recipe Notes	133
Recipe Notes	135
Recipe Notes	137
Recipe Notes	139
Acknowledgments	141
Books by Deborah Garner	143

For my mother,
who always made holidays special for us.

Chapter One

Mist looked out the window at the falling snow, watching it float softly to the ground. She rocked from side to side, arms crossed in front of her, as the white blanket already covering the front yard received the fresh new layer.

"More snow today, Rain," she whispered to the sweet bundle she held lovingly against her. "Isn't that wonderful? Our guests will be so pleased to have a white Christmas." She kissed the baby's head, amazed, just as she was every minute of every day, that the precious girl had come into the world almost five months ago. It filled her with a sense of awe she'd never known was possible. She'd always felt the world was filled with wonder, but nothing matched this.

"Let's go see what Betty's up to," she suggested as she turned away from the winter scene and headed for the kitchen. She stepped around the elegant Christmas tree that stood in front of the window, having slipped around its side in order to enjoy the view of the snow. Crossing beneath the festive garland of pine branches and red satin ribbons that adorned the archway between the front parlor and foyer, she passed through the café lovingly known as the Moonglow Café and entered the kitchen, where she found Betty sipping coffee at the center island.

Betty perked up at the sight of the baby. "How's our little girl today?"

"Right as Rain." Mist smiled. It was her usual response to the question; one she couldn't resist. The name Rain had been the only one that felt right when the sweet child entered the world. In fact, it had felt right months before that. Fortunately, Michael, the proud father, had agreed. Though some took it as a poetic complement to Mist's own name, this had never been part of the decision. The name had simply felt like the right one.

"Another Christmas holiday is here," Betty said. "My favorite time of year."

Mist took a seat across from Betty, allowing enough room between the seat and the counter for Rain to rest comfortably in front of her. She'd been thrilled to find the soft organic cotton fabric with a moon-and-star print when she'd made the baby wrap earlier in the year. Designed so Rain could either face her or face forward, it was the saving grace that let her accomplish many of the hotel and café tasks.

"I was looking at the registration book earlier," Betty said as she tapped a binder in the center of the island. "You're good at finding out a little bit about them when they make their reservation. Who do we have this year? Aside from the regulars, of course."

The delight of regular visitors arriving each year had been established over many years. Clara and Andrew would be there, as always, and of course the professor. Michael had been considered a regular guest for a long time, but now that he and Mist were married and lived just a few doors away, he'd earned the status of local townsfolk.

Mist pulled the book closer and flipped it open. "We have a music professor from Missoula, Wesley Palmer, who teaches at the university. The professor knows him. He and his wife, Elisa, will be staying here along with their daughter."

"A young daughter?"

"Not too young, I think. Maybe preteen?"

"That'll be nice." Betty smiled and then took a sip of coffee. "I always love having children here during the holidays."

"I do too. It lets us see Christmas through their eyes," Mist mused.

"And the two adults have extended a delightful offer. They'd like to serenade the Christmas Eve dinner with acoustic guitar music."

"How wonderful! But they will have dinner too," Betty said. "Won't they?"

"We'll make sure of it."

"Who else will be here this year?" Betty leaned forward as if to read the list of names, although the book was upside down from her place at the counter.

Mist ran her finger down the page. "We'll have Scarlet Brady from Washington state, just outside Spokane. I know she said she'd be driving here. And we also have Giulia and Tommaso Bernardi. They're coming all the way from Tuscany, and I recall her saying Clara and Andrew had recommended us. Somehow they all know each other. It'll be fun to find out how."

"Lovely." Betty smiled. "We'll have to thank them for the referral."

Approaching footsteps were followed by Clive's enthusiastic appearance in the kitchen. Though it was often fresh-baked goods that drew him, this had changed over the past five months. To everyone's surprise and delight, he had assumed the role of unofficial doting grandfather. There was no keeping him away from Rain, and his animated theatrics around the baby were a constant source of comedy. True to his current modus operandi, he walked right past a tray of apple-cinnamon muffins as if they didn't exist.

"There she is!" Clive beamed as he reached out to pinch the baby's cheeks. "How's my favorite girl today?"

Mist and Betty exchanged amused glances, and Betty rolled her eyes. "That used to be me," she said with a wink. She stood up and headed to the coffeepot. She refilled her cup, poured a second one for Clive, and returned to her seat with both.

"That's still you, my dear." Clive gave Betty a peck on the cheek and sat down beside her. He took a sip of coffee, thanked Betty for it, and then waved to Rain, making faces at the same time. In response, Rain smiled and giggled. Clive and the sweet girl had developed a delightful bond over the past five months.

"What are you up to today?" Betty waved a hand in front of Clive's face to get his attention.

"I told Duffy I'd stop by to help him cut a few more angel ornaments. He got a new shipment of balsa wood in."

"Maisie has more ribbon for them," Mist said. "She's dropping it off today since they were running low. Millie adds ribbon to each after they're decorated."

"I love this ornament project," Betty said. "The idea of making two ornaments, one to keep and one to give away, is so clever. People have been having such fun deciding who to give the second one to. Marge sent one to a nephew who's deployed overseas."

"It'll be interesting to see where others went," Mist said. "Near, far, so many options."

Clive finished his coffee and stood. "I'd better run by the gallery before heading to Duffy's. The new part-timer, Addison, is fantastic. She can handle the place on her own. But I don't want her to think I've deserted her." He rounded the counter and leaned in toward Rain, offering a bit of baby talk chatter before heading out.

Betty also stood. "And I have things to do around the hotel here. The guests are arriving tomorrow, not today, right?" She looked at Mist.

Mist nodded. "Yes, all on the same day this year. It'll be a little hectic, but they'll arrive at different times. And it gives us today to relax and prepare. Maisie will be by soon with flowers to make arrangements. We'll work on those together, the two of us."

"The *four* of you," Betty qualified, knowing anytime Mist and Maisie got together now, there would be two very young helpers with them.

"Yes." Mist smiled. "Rain and Cora will be very helpful. Especially Cora since she's a month older."

At this statement, Mist and Betty both laughed. They could only imagine the trouble two infants could get into. Wishing each other a good day, they took off for their various tasks.

Chapter Two

One thing Mist could always count on for the holidays was a beautiful assortment of fresh flowers and greenery to use for the café. Creating centerpieces for the tables and arrangements for the buffet was one of the highlights of the season for her. And it was more than a little serendipitous that her closest friend owned the local flower shop, Maisie's Daisies. This year Maisie had brought in a fabulous variety, which now awaited a magic touch. Roses in rich red and elegant ivory rested on the café tables with paperwhites, orchids, winterberries, splashes of greenery, and other elements in mixed textures: holly, evergreen branches, eucalyptus, pine cones.

Mist had planned, as she always did, to keep table centerpieces low in order to let guests comfortably converse with each other over their meals. She'd been delighted to find shallow glass dishes that would work nicely for the arrangements this year. They weren't fancy, but that wasn't important. They were a good six inches across and just under two inches in height, providing an easy base that was wide enough for a creative assortment. Mist felt sure she'd use most of what Maisie had provided. It felt like a year to be creative, maybe use combinations she hadn't used in the past. So much about life felt new.

"I see you found everything," Maisie said, arriving by way of the kitchen's doorway. Mist looked up and smiled. She and Maisie were practically regarded as twins these days, each having given birth in late summer, each to girls. This delighted just about everyone in town, especially Mist and Maisie themselves as they looked forward to the two girls growing up together.

"Look who's here, Rain!" Mist said. "It's Cora. She's come to help us today!"

Maisie set Cora's chair next to Rain's, which was already settled nearby. Although the two girls noticed each other, it was funny to watch them try to figure the situation out.

"Don't you wonder what they're thinking sometimes?" Maisie asked.

"All the time." Mist held an ivory rose up with a branch of winterberries, admiring the contrast. She set it aside and chose greenery to go with it. "I'm thinking mosaics."

"Hmm?" Maisie asked, turning away from the girls and taking a seat. "I'd love to help. What kind of mosaics?"

"Flower mosaics, and I would love doing this together," Mist said, taking one of the glass dishes and setting it next to the foliage. "Imagine this dish is a tray and you plan to place small chips of color on it to create a mosaic pattern. We'll do the same thing, but we'll use flowers and greenery."

"Like a collage," Maisie said.

"Yes, that would be another way to think of it. A flat design, although not completely flat in this case because we're working with textures and shapes." Mist demonstrated by placing a rose next to paperwhites in the glass dish, stems cut short.

"I get it," Maisie said. "And they don't all have to be the same?"

"Heavens no," Mist said. "Each one can be different. That's part of the charm. Let's see what we get. I'll make one, and you make one, and then we'll compare, see how inspiration strikes."

"I know they'll both be lovely," Maisie said.

Mist laughed. "I suspect you have an advantage, seeing as you own the flower shop! But it's not a competition. Just have fun."

Over the next hour and a half, counting breaks for peppermint tea and keeping the babies entertained, Mist and Maisie created enough floral centerpieces to grace each table in the café as well as one for the registration desk in the lobby. One larger arrangement—taller and longer—was set aside for the buffet.

"A job well done," Maisie proclaimed as she stood and prepared to leave. She gathered Cora into her arms and grasped the baby's chair with one hand.

"I don't know how you manage to move around so easily with her," Mist said, admiring Maisie's easy manner with Cora.

Maisie laughed. "I think it's called 'this is not the first child.'"

"That's a good point."

"Absolutely," Maisie said. "I was nervous with Clay Jr. because everything was new. Don't worry, Mist. You're doing great. We learn as we go."

Thanking Maisie for her help as well as her wisdom, Mist lifted Rain into her arms and moved to the closet in the back hallway where she kept her secret stash of trinkets to place in the guest rooms. Some were designed to amuse, some were intended to inspire creativity, and some aimed to distract from the cares of the world. Each was a found treasure, whether from a yard sale, thrift shop, or other location. Mist never knew where she might find items that intrigued her. But she knew when she found them.

As to which items would go into which rooms, she chose by instinct. And so she now rummaged through bins and baskets, tubs and tins, eventually arriving at an assortment to place in the rooms: a collection of miniature ceramic farm animals, a tin of loose beads, a vintage Nancy Drew book, a stamp collection album with loose stamps not yet added, a plush moose with a bright red bow around its neck.

She gathered her choices into a pile just outside the closet, closed the door, and headed to the kitchen, where she found Betty enjoying a cup of coffee at the center island.

"How would you like to hold this little angel for the next sixty seconds?"

Betty clapped her hands and reached out. "I would love to!"

Mist let Rain move into Betty's arms and then slipped back into the hallway, returning only a minute later with her arms full.

"Oh, you have your trinket choices for this year! Let's see!" Betty leaned forward as Mist placed the items on the counter.

"This was my favorite book of this series," Mist said, holding up the copy of *The Secret of the Hidden Staircase*. "I must have read it a dozen times." She handed the book to Betty, trading it for Rain. She settled the baby into the moon-and-stars wrap.

"I loved Nancy Drew books too." Betty flipped through the pages. "I was quite a reader back then. I'm not sure how I got out of the habit."

"It's never too late to get back into it. Millie has a great selection of books at the library," Mist hinted. "I bet you even have a library card."

Betty nodded. "Indeed, I do. Maybe I'll take a walk over

there and pick something out. A Christmas tale maybe. Something seasonal."

"Why don't I go with you?" Mist suggested. "I've been wanting to swing by there to see what's new in the used-book sale area. I just need to drop these odds and ends off in the rooms."

Creating a library in the house she and Michael now shared had been an ongoing project, one that brought them both great joy. Though the space available was only a small alcove off the side of the living room, they'd managed to construct floor-to-ceiling shelving to fill with Michael's collection of classics as well as a growing assortment of children's books. This had been a special activity of Mist's as she anticipated Rain's arrival. Both she and Michael agreed it was never too early to start reading to a child. As a result, the five-month-old had heard over one hundred stories, though undoubtedly not understanding a single one.

A trip to the library, followed by a peaceful evening at home with Michael and Rain, was a perfect plan. Because, as anyone familiar with Christmas at the Timberton Hotel would know, the next few days would be anything but quiet.

Chapter Three

Mist took care as she stepped from the house in the morning and headed to the hotel. The chilly wind and icy sidewalk led her to tread carefully. Though she'd kept a room in the hotel where she could always stay during busy times—and certainly the holidays were such—she'd chosen to stay at home every night after Rain was born even though it meant very early morning walks. And so now, at just past five a.m., she walked the half block that separated home from work and let herself quietly into the hotel. Michael would follow in a few hours with Rain, but for now she had time on her own.

She relished these quiet hours when she could prepare fresh-baked goods and have time to think. Being alone at the beginning of the day helped her put the day in order—what tasks needed attending, what food would be prepared, which guests would be arriving, and what the likely timing of all of it would be. As she fixed herself a cup of tea and began to mix ingredients for cranberry scones, she reviewed plans for the rest of the day. In this case, it involved serving a simple breakfast in the café, then greeting the guest arrivals, then hopefully a trip to Duffy's to see how the angel ornament project was going, and then offering another meal in the café that evening. It would be a busy day but fulfilling, which made it all worthwhile.

Everything she did for the hotel or town felt like a blessing, more for herself than for anyone else, though many would argue with that. There were times when she wondered how she could possibly have ended up so lucky. She'd found the perfect town, the perfect job, the perfect partner, and certainly the perfect miniature of herself, which is how close friends described Rain. She could create art, could delight in preparing culinary feasts, could breathe in the clean mountain air, and could bask in the peaceful town ambiance. It was a perfect life in so many ways, and she was eternally grateful for it.

After sliding a batch of cranberry scones into the oven, she moved on to arranging the beverage table in the front lobby. She set the coffee to brew along with a large carafe of hot water for those who might prefer tea or hot chocolate. After adding assorted tea bags, cream, and sugar to the table, she created an open space for the warm scones she would soon bring out.

Returning to the kitchen, she checked the oven and determined the scones needed just a few minutes more. She passed that time reviewing her notes in the registration book until the needed time went by, and she pulled the baked goods from the oven to begin to cool. Checking her notes one last time, she closed the registration book, content. Yes, they were ready for all the guests to arrive.

Mist heard the front door open and close softly, followed by a pair of low voices. She smiled, knowing this would be Clive and Duffy sneaking in for coffee. This had been Clive's habit for years, but he and the relatively new store owner had formed a friendship during the year since the shop, aptly named Duffy's, opened. It was good to see Clive enjoy Duffy's company as well as for Duffy, a relative newcomer to Timberton, to have a friend in town.

Placing scones, fresh from the oven, into a small basket, Mist took them out to the front parlor and added them to the beverage table, much to the delight of both men.

"Well, look at that!" Clive exclaimed, picking up one of the scones as Duffy did the same. "It's like magic around here. And they're warm too."

"Indeed they are," Duffy said. "I keep trying to get her to make some for the store but to no avail." He winked at Mist.

Clive nodded, playing along with a joke they'd bantered back and forth before. "It's as if running the café, helping Betty manage the hotel, providing artwork for the gallery, and taking care of a newborn occupies all her time."

"Imagine that," Duffy said, shaking his head. "I reckon she oughta have lots of free time left over, don't you?" He took a bite of the scone, closed his eyes, and sighed with approval.

"Yep," Clive chirped. "That's the way I see it."

A new voice joined the conversation as Betty emerged from the kitchen and stood next to Mist. "You two ruffians aren't giving Mist a hard time, are you? Again?" Betty's smile made it clear she was teasing, but the overall comment was valid.

"There is a possible answer to this dilemma," Mist said, a sparkle in her eyes. "If you really want those scones in the store."

"Oh yeah?" Duffy's eyes lit up.

"I'll just stop making food for the café and just bake for Duffy's instead," Mist proclaimed with an impish smile. Betty, not having heard the first part of the discussion, raised both eyebrows.

Clive and Duffy shook their heads dramatically, just as Mist knew they would. Many of the town residents depended on the Moonglow Café for food. Those who couldn't eat at the café for various reasons, whether lack of funds or mobility challenges, often found "leftovers" on their doorstep, the result of some intentional overproduction.

"That's what I thought," Mist said. Betty let out a sigh of relief, although she knew Mist's comment had been in jest.

Clive reached for another scone in spite of not having finished the first. "I'd better take another one with me. The gallery is going to be busy today with Christmas shoppers." He smiled at Mist. "Your miniature paintings are flying out of there as usual. Thank you for making so many in advance this year."

Mist had learned over the past few years that the gallery often needed additional paintings just before Christmas. This year, between all the hotel activity and Rain's presence on top of it all, planning ahead had become crucial. She'd used slightly quieter months—in particular, the months before Rain came into the world—to complete as many miniature paintings as she could. This included her regular designs of winter forest scenes, pine cone clusters, and more, as well as several new designs: stars above a field of snow, a vintage sleigh filled with evergreen boughs, and a fairy-tale cottage.

"Your custom jewelry is also selling well, Clive," Betty reminded him. "As well as the silver ornaments with Yogo sapphires." Years ago, Clive had started designing an ornament for Betty each year. She'd finally convinced him a few years back to make them for his customers too. They were an immediate hit.

Duffy made a huffing sound. "Well, not to outdo you artsy people, but I do have peppermint ice cream in the soda fountain this week." He blew on his fingers and rubbed them near his shoulder, feigning importance.

"Don't make light of that," Betty said. "I bet if you just counted sales, you might sell more of those than the paintings and jewelry combined."

"She's right," Clive said.

"Did I hear that correctly?" Betty whispered to Mist.

Clive cleared his throat. "As I was saying, Betty is right. Those peppermint ice-cream sodas are a perfect treat for the season. I'm assuming this, of course. I still need to stop by and do some testing. Maybe later today."

"You're mighty welcome to," Duffy said. "I might even give you a discount."

With that, Clive and Duffy took their leave, along with two cups of coffee and several cranberry scones. Shaking their heads, Mist and Betty returned to the kitchen to finish preparing for the day.

Chapter Four

Michael came by the hotel with Rain to allow some mother-daughter time before guests began to arrive. A casual breakfast of oatmeal, fresh berries, and cranberry scones provided a start to the day. A few townsfolk stopped by to partake of the same, but they quickly moved on to holiday errands and other tasks to be done. Michael finished breakfast while Mist and Rain sauntered around the front parlor, talking about... well, whatever they talked about. That was the only way Michael could describe it. Part talking, part singing, part imagining. Mist and Rain seemed to have a communication system all their own, something that not only Michael but just about everyone found enchanting.

Michael helped Betty clean up the few breakfast dishes and then took over Rain duty again, telling the sweet baby that they were "going to see Grandpa Clive," a statement that always resulted in a chuckle or two when overheard. He thanked Mist and Betty for breakfast and headed out to Clive's gallery.

Betty and Mist were in the process of sprucing up the front

parlor—Mist setting up hot mulled cider in the beverage area while Betty refilled a crystal dish of glazed cinnamon nuts—when the front door opened and a couple in their late thirties entered. Mist knew immediately that it was Elisa and Wesley Palmer.

"Welcome to the Timberton Hotel," Mist said. "We're delighted to have you spending Christmas with us. And your daughter is with you, I believe?" Mist looked around. There was no sign of a child.

Elisa sighed. "That would be Kylie. She's in the car, refusing to come in."

"She wasn't too keen about coming on this trip," Wesley explained. "Having to be away from her friends. So there's a bit of an attitude going on."

"It's the tween years, I suppose," Elisa offered as further explanation. "Though I think these days eleven should be placed directly in the teen category. Maybe just call it 'eleven-teen' instead of eleven."

Mist smiled. "I understand. I wouldn't worry. We're quite good with that sort of situation here, especially during the holidays. There's a certain type of magic in the air this time of year."

"Well, that's good to hear!" Elisa said.

"I'll go get her." Wesley started for the front door but looked back at the sound of Mist's voice.

"Why don't I go talk to her?"

"I can help you with registration in the meantime," Betty offered. "We have you in a suite that will allow you all some space."

Mist watched as the parents exchanged glances and nodded. Seeing the sign of approval, she lifted her favorite burgundy cape off the corner coatrack, wrapped it around her shoulders, and stepped outside.

The crisp December air caressed her face, invigorating compared to the warmth inside the hotel. She'd always found winter to be an exhilarating season in many ways, and she relished the sensation on her skin as she descended the front steps.

It was clear which car belonged to the Palmer family. Not only was it parked right in front of the hotel, but the windows were slightly steamed up, essentially guaranteeing the presence of a living being inside. Circling the car, Mist debated which seat the child might be in. Gambling on the back seat, passenger side, she chose that door for her approach.

Softly she tapped on the window as if she were knocking on the front door of someone's house. "Hello?"

Hearing no answer, she repeated the gesture. "Hello? Anyone home?" This resulted in a hint of movement on the other side of the fogged glass. Yet there was no reply. Pondering her options, Mist circled the car and arrived at the opposite door. Feeling an impulse of initiative, she opened the door, slid onto the seat, and closed the door again.

As expected, the seat across from her was occupied by a girl matching the age her mother had referenced. She was bundled up in a bright green winter coat, mittens that appeared to be hand-knit in a forest leaf print, and a heavy scarf of a lighter shade of green than her coat. A few red curls poked out of a knit cap that matched her mittens and fit snugly over her head and ears.

Rather than start into a conversation right away, Mist simply sat and waited for a reaction from the young guest, which she soon got.

"Are you always this weird?" The girl took a slight peek at Mist while speaking though didn't turn to face her completely.

"Not always," Mist said. "Just sometimes." It was a true enough statement. She'd never been directly accused of being weird, at least not to her face. But she'd frequently heard herself referred to as "just a little different." She took it as a compliment, just as she might consider weird to be. And weird was a relative term after all.

The girl blew a puff of air up toward her forehead to move a stray curl out of one eye. "Well, it seems pretty weird to me to get in a stranger's car."

Mist nodded. "I guess you're right. But it seems pretty weird to me to stay in a car when there's a warm hotel just a few steps away."

"Whatever."

Mist knew better than to try to disagree with the ephemeral sentiment of "whatever." It was a transient state of mind that was bound to be replaced soon by something more substantial. In this case, the hope was that a desire to go inside would follow. She glanced at the girl and noticed that while her expression was steadfast in resolve, her body was less so. She was beginning to shiver.

"I could sure use a mug of hot chocolate about now," Mist said. She let the suggestion hover in the chilly air. "With marshmallows, I think." She tapped her chin as if thinking this over. "Yes, marshmallows, lots of tiny ones."

"And a peppermint stick?" Kylie turned part of the way toward Mist.

"Oh, absolutely!" Mist nodded enthusiastically. "What good is hot chocolate without a peppermint stick?"

"You have hot chocolate in there?" Kylie glanced at the hotel as if reconsidering its merits.

"Always. And cookies. And plenty of other treats." Mist let that sink in and then followed it up with a final card. "It's also warm and cozy. We have a great fireplace. I don't like being too cold."

"Yeah, same here." Kylie pulled her jacket tighter around her neck. "Maybe we should go inside."

"If you think so," Mist said casually.

"I do think so," Kylie replied as she regarded the hotel again. "It's pretty cold out here. Let's go inside."

Mist smiled. "I think that's a great idea."

Chapter Five

CLIVE POPPED HIS HEAD AROUND THE KITCHEN DOOR. "Clara and Andrew have arrived. They're coming up the walkway. I'm sure they're anxious to see Rain!" He disappeared as quickly as he had appeared but immediately stuck his head back in. "And you too, of course, Mist!" Again he ducked back out, this time out the side door in order to gather logs for the fireplace in the front parlor.

Mist looked at Betty and let out a dramatic mock sigh. "I remember there was a time when people arrived anxious to see *us*, Betty."

Betty laughed. "I'm sorry to be the one to tell you this, but no one can compete with a cute baby. Besides, Clara and Andrew have been coming here for ages. They're like family."

"They *are* family," Mist said. "They're part of the lovely holiday family that gathers here each year."

"Just think of them as an aunt and uncle seeing their niece for the first time," Betty suggested. "I can't wait to see their faces!"

"Shall we go meet them?" Mist directed this to the baby in

question, who was snuggled against her in a soothing sage-green wrap. She received a gurgle of sorts in reply, which she took to be a yes. She kissed the baby's head and walked out to the front lobby, passing through the café on the way. Betty followed.

Clara beamed at the sight of Mist, Rain, and Betty emerging from the café. Andrew clapped his hands together, equally excited. The senior couple looked healthy and well with good color to their faces and smiles that said they were ecstatic to be there. Mist and Betty mirrored their enthusiasm.

"Well, look at you!" Clara exclaimed as she gave Mist an awkward hug. She then turned all her attention to Rain, oohing and aahing and letting the baby grasp her finger. Andrew signed the registration card while that was going on and then greeted Mist and Rain while Clara said hello to Betty.

"We're so glad to have you here," Betty said. "Your room is all ready. I can't wait to catch up, especially to know where you two took your annual trip this year." The tradition had started years ago. Clara and Andrew took a trip each year to a different location, sometimes domestic, sometimes international. Tales of their recent excursions—Hawaii, the Netherlands, and the pyramids in Egypt—had been fascinating to hear.

"Can't wait to tell you about it!" Clara exclaimed. "We went to Tuscany this year, and it was fabulous. We'll tell you more once we get settled."

Clive joined them, arriving with arms full of wood. Nigel Hennessy—better known to everyone as the professor—was right behind him.

"Will you look at that?" Clive said, shaking hands with Andrew after setting the wood down by the fireplace. "I guess they let anyone in here."

Andrew laughed. "Yes, and it's a good thing. There's

nowhere we'd rather be for the holidays. Good to see you, Clive, and you too, Nigel."

"I hope you're ready for our yearly chess match," the professor quipped.

"Absolutely," Andrew said. "I can see that checkmate in my future already."

"Then I apologize in advance."

"Not exactly what I meant!" Andrew replied. Both men laughed, the competitive spirit alive and well.

The professor turned to Betty and Mist in greeting, and he smiled at Rain. Living just up the road a hundred miles or so, where he taught at the university, he'd already been to visit several times since Rain was born. He was always charmed to see her, and he especially enjoyed giving Clive a hard time about his adopted doting grandfather role.

"I'll take the suitcases up," Andrew offered. He turned toward Mist. "Same room as usual?"

"Of course." Mist smiled. She knew guests enjoyed having the same accommodations each time they returned. Familiarity was comforting. Clara, in particular, was fond of a quilt that Mist made sure was always in that room, just as she made sure the professor's PG Tips tea and McVitie's Digestives were waiting for him.

The front door opened yet again, and a flurry of excited greetings suddenly filled the air. Mist and Betty both stepped back to watch the hugs and cheers as Clara and Andrew greeted the new arrivals.

"You're here!" Clara exclaimed.

"*Certo!* Of course! You knew we were coming!" The petite thirty-something woman removed a red knit cap to reveal short brown hair with wisps of golden highlights. Her eyes matched her hair right down to tiny gold flecks. She smiled as she stepped forward to embrace Clara.

"I did!" Clara laughed. "I just knew I wouldn't believe it until I saw it, but here you are. In the United States. In Montana. In Timberton!"

"Good to see you." Andrew set down the suitcase and exchanged handshakes and hugs.

"Come meet our wonderful hosts." Clara gestured toward Mist and Betty.

"You must be Giulia and Tommaso Bernardi," Mist said. "We're so pleased to have you here."

"Thank you," Tommaso, a striking man of medium height with dark hair, olive skin, and strong facial features, said. "Just Tom is fine for me." Only a hint of Italian accent came through, his English impeccable.

"We're delighted to be here. And this is for you," Giulia said, handing Betty a gift since Mist's arms were full. "It's Pannetone from Florence, a Christmas tradition." Giulia noted the baby in Mist's arms and offered a smile that struck Mist as friendly yet slightly reserved.

"All the way from Tuscany. How wonderful!" Betty set a registration card on the desk while Andrew introduced Clive and the professor, who'd been watching the animated arrival.

"Tuscany, one of my favorite places in the world," the professor said. "Brilliant in so many ways."

"I take it you've been there," Tom said.

"Yes, we used to go there on holiday when I was young." The professor turned to the others. "That would be 'vacation' to most of you."

"Ah, I think I recognize that accent," Tom mused. "London, isn't it?"

"Right-o," the professor quipped. "Though I live here now."

Clive stepped forward and clapped his hands together twice, just enough to catch the attention of the various newcomers. "Why don't I help some of you with your bags? Mist can tell us who goes where, and we'll get you situated."

"Excellent idea," Andrew said. "We'll have plenty of time to catch up later."

"Yes," Mist said. "Over dinner which, for those of you here for the first time, will be served in the café." She indicated the Moonglow Café, just off the lobby.

"As well as time to relax and visit in the front parlor later on," Betty added.

Giulia and Tom looked at each other and nodded. Giulia filled out the registration card while Clara and Andrew proceeded upstairs to their room. The professor tutted that he'd see everyone at dinner and headed upstairs as well.

Once keys were all distributed and guests were on their way to get settled in, Mist and Betty looked at each other with a sense of accomplishment.

"Well, we're going to have a full house," Betty said. "And a lively one at that!"

"You're right, Betty." Mist swayed back and forth to calm Rain, who had started to fuss. "A full house, indeed. And we wouldn't want it any other way."

Chapter Six

Michael entered the kitchen, assessed the scene, and laughed. "I should take a picture of this." He pulled a cell phone from his pocket and followed through. Rain sat in the middle of the center island, content in her baby chair, a tray of diced tomatoes, carrots, and peppers to one side and a bowl of fresh herbs to the other. "If she's not actually helping prepare the meal, maybe I could take her into the living room and watch her. I'm just going to read by the fireplace."

"I would love that," Mist admitted. "I need to chop and sauté onions and garlic, and I don't think those will be new favorite smells for her. I'd also love to pop down to Duffy's and see how the angel ornament project is going. Maybe you could check the stove for me while I'm there? Just one pot simmering."

"Not a problem," Michael said.

"Will you be reading for a while?"

"It's Tolstoy."

"Okay then," Mist quipped. "I'll see you in a week or two."

"Very funny. Why don't I keep her for a couple of hours, let you get some things done." He picked up the sweet baby from the counter, chair included, maneuvering both around the bowl of herbs. She cooed sweetly as she eased into her father's arms.

"Two hours would be fantastic," Mist admitted. "Though you know I adore every second with her."

"I know you do," Michael said, giving her a soft kiss on her neck. "But you have several days of guest activities to handle. Besides, it's never too early to introduce someone to Russian literature." He looked at Rain. "Isn't that right? Let's go see what Anna Karenina is up to."

Mist rolled her eyes, which Betty caught, having entered at the same time as Michael was exiting.

"And what was that about?" Betty smiled. "It's always something curious when you roll your eyes, a rare gesture for you."

"Russian literature and babies," Mist said.

"I guess that's supposed to make sense." Betty took a seat at the island counter. "Is Rain signing up for literature classes? Wouldn't she want to start with board books and move on to chapter books before hitting the heavy stuff?"

Mist laughed. "Ask Michael. This is what she gets for having a literature teacher for a father."

"That could turn out to be a good thing," Betty suggested.

"Indeed. As long as her first word isn't Dostoyevsky, I won't worry."

"So he's keeping her for a while today?"

Mist nodded. "Yes. Long enough that I can finish up here and go by Duffy's. I want to see how the angel ornaments are coming along."

"Oh, I'd love to go with you," Betty said. "It's wonderful the way Duffy turned the front of the soda fountain space into a community project area."

"It has helped Millie to not have to host every town project and activity at the library. And I doubt it hurts his soda fountain sales either."

"I imagine you're right!" Betty chuckled.

Mist finished chopping, dribbled extra virgin olive oil into a large stock pot, and dropped the onion and garlic in. As that began to sizzle, she eased the diced veggies in along with a dozen other ingredients, fresh herbs included. "I'm almost done. I'll set this up for a couple of hours of simmering, and then we can go. Michael will check on it."

"Is this what you're serving tonight in the café?" Betty asked as she regarded the ingredients in the pot. "It smells delicious."

"Yes. Something simple," Mist said, "as is typical for the days leading up to the big Christmas Eve feast."

Betty laughed. "Your idea of simple is not necessarily other people's idea of simple. Spill it."

"Veggie chili, a salad, jalapeño cornbread, and blueberry cobbler."

"Sounds delicious," Betty said.

"It'll make an easy buffet," Mist said as she adjusted the temperature for the burner.

"And for the not-exactly-simple Christmas Eve meal this year? You haven't told me what you finally decided on." Betty tapped her fingers on the counter.

"Since you asked..." Mist slid a paper to her with a list of dishes in calligraphy-type print. "This is the final menu."

- *Roast turkey with apple-cranberry stuffing*
- *Balsamic glazed salmon*
- *Portobello mushroom wellington*
- *Asian pear salad with peanut-lime dressing*
- *Rice pilaf with lemony brown-butter mushrooms*
- *Parmesan herb-roasted acorn squash*

- *Crispy leaf potatoes with butter, rosemary, and salt.*
- *Pecan pie with champagne ice cream*

"Oh my!" Betty exclaimed. "I'm afraid I have a dilemma."

"And what is that?" Mist stirred the stock pot and adjusted the temperature.

"I don't know how I'll manage to taste everything and still have room for three servings of pecan pie and champagne ice cream at the end."

Mist grinned. "I see. You do have a dilemma there."

"What dilemma am I hearing?" Clive's voice broke into the conversation as he stepped into the kitchen.

"The same one you're going to have! Look at this!" Betty waved the paper in front of him and stood by while he read it. She watched his eyes get bigger. "How will I have room for extra dessert?"

"That's an easy one," Clive said, setting the paper back on the counter. "I'll eat more of the roast turkey, the rice whatever-that-is, and the crispy potatoes."

"*Pilaf*," Mist whispered.

"Right, that," Clive said, winking at Mist before turning back to Betty. "And then you can have that pear salad and the veggies, and you'll have plenty of room for pie and ice cream." Clive took a bow as if having solved a global conundrum.

Betty gave him a kiss on the cheek. "You're very clever, my dear."

"I know. I mean, thank you." He pretended to wince as Betty smacked him playfully on the arm.

"I plan to have some of that salmon too," Betty said. "That's a fun addition to this year's holiday menu."

"That was Michael's suggestion," Mist said. "Or more specifically, the professor's suggestion passed on through Michael. We have guests from Italy this year, and—according to the professor—it's a tradition in Italy to have seafood on Christmas Eve."

"Oh, I've heard of that," Betty said. "The Feast of Seven Fishes, right?"

Mist smiled. "Yes, but here it will be the Feast of One Fish." A sound followed from Mist that sounded surprisingly like a giggle.

"As usual, there's something for everyone on your menus," Betty said. "It'll be a splendid feast indeed, as always."

Clive headed for the side door. "I'm going down to Duffy's to see if he needs any more help. He was going to try to cut another fifty ornaments."

"We were just talking about going to check on those," Betty said. "We'll see you there in a bit." She turned back to Mist.

"I'm ready." Mist stirred the pot of chili one more time and set the spoon aside on a spoon rest shaped like a gingerbread house. "Let's go out the front so I can wave to Michael. That way he'll know we're leaving. He'll keep an eye on the stove between reading passages."

"Reading passages you say?" Betty quirked an eyebrow.

Mist smiled. "You'll see."

As they passed through the front lobby and acquired outerwear—a cape for Mist and a jacket for Betty—they overheard one of many quotes that Michael would read to Rain that afternoon.

"She knew that in politics, in philosophy, in theology, Alexey Alexandrovitch often had doubts and made investigations; but on questions of art and poetry, and, above all, of music, of which he was totally devoid of understanding, he had the most distinct and decided opinions. He was fond of talking about Shakespeare, Raphael, Beethoven, of the significance of new schools of poetry and music, all of which were classified by him with very conspicuous consistency."

Betty stifled a laugh in order to not interrupt the sweet scene. "I see what you mean. At this rate, she'll be teaching at the university right alongside Michael by the time she graduates kindergarten."

Mist didn't even bother to hide her laugh, partially because she wanted to alert Michael to the fact they were leaving. "I don't doubt it."

"Is this really what he reads to her?" Betty whispered.

Mist lowered her voice to match Betty's. "Don't worry. He's only amusing himself. Tonight it'll be *Pat the Bunny* or *Barnyard Bedtime*."

"I see." Betty smiled.

Both women waved to Michael, who acknowledged their departure. He returned to reading, and Mist and Betty headed for Duffy's.

Chapter Seven

A TRIP TO DUFFY'S WAS ALWAYS JOYFUL. THE AMBIANCE the lovely man had created when he opened the store a year ago fit perfectly into the charming town atmosphere of Timberton. Part practical—groceries and other household necessities—part whimsical—vintage toys and handmade wooden knickknacks—and part nostalgia—a soda fountain and old-fashioned photos of the town on the walls, it was immediately embraced by the community.

Mist and Betty arrived at the store after a brief stop to visit with Marge at the candy store. Betty couldn't help but pick up a few of her favorite caramels, and Mist chose a cluster of ribboned peppermint sticks to leave on Kylie's door.

Duffy's storefront announced the season with enthusiasm. Poinsettias lined the entrance, and the front windows boasted a holiday extravaganza complete with trimmed Christmas tree, stockings, and a train running merrily around the entire display.

"I adore these," Mist said, indicating a scattered assortment of birdhouses hanging under a front awning. "So many styles and shapes, all rustic yet with bits of color here and there—a red roof, a blue windowsill, a yellow weathervane."

"He loves working with wood," Betty pointed out.

"It's a good thing," Mist said as she held the door open for Betty. "It's the reason we have the angel ornaments for people to decorate."

"He and Clive have been having a good time making them, though I suspect telling tall tales might be part of their agenda." Betty laughed. "Which is fine. I'm glad Duffy and Clive have formed a friendship."

"Is this not partially because it keeps Clive out of your hair sometimes?" Mist said teasingly.

"Well, yes," Betty admitted, chuckling. "That too!"

Once inside, Betty headed to a barrel of wrapping paper rolls, having spotted Glenda from the Curl 'n' Cue debating between styles. Leaving Betty to visit, Mist passed through the front of the store and into the adjacent room where an old-fashioned soda fountain sat to the right and a large craft table sat to the left. Millie, the town librarian, was in the process of monitoring the table's impressive supply of balsa wood angels, paint, glitter, feathers, and more.

"How's it going?" Mist asked.

"Wonderfully!" Millie exclaimed. "The idea of making one ornament to keep and one to give away was fabulous. You should hear some of the stories people are telling me as they're making these."

Mist smiled, silently pleased that the project was giving people a reason to think of someone to give their second angel ornament to. Some would know immediately; others would have a chance to think about people in their lives that they might have overlooked recently, as is not uncommon during busy lives.

"Has anyone done more than two?" Mist asked.

"Oh yes!" Millie exclaimed. "Just this morning a child made one for herself and one for each set of grandparents. One angel held a tray of cookies because the child said that her grandfather likes to sneak cookies from the kitchen when the grandmother isn't looking. And the other angel held a small white poodle, or so she said. The child was five, so you can imagine the designs were a little abstract."

Mist laughed. "I can imagine. All a part of the magic of children."

"Speaking of children and angels, where is your little angel today?"

"Michael has her. He's been especially wonderful about doing more during the holiday season when the hotel is full. And Rain adores him; she's always content when she's with him." Mist looked around. Seeing Betty still in conversation with Glenda, she turned back to the craft table.

"Millie, have you had a break at all?"

"Who needs a break from something this delightful?" Still, Millie considered Mist's offer. "Now that you mention it, I'd love to walk a bit, stretch my legs, maybe accidentally pass by the soda fountain."

"Perfect. I'll cover." Mist gently shooed Millie away and took a seat behind the craft table. Perusing the supplies, she couldn't help but pick up a blank ornament and paintbrush. Choosing a rich gold color, she neatly applied the paint to the lightweight wood and then sprinkled gold glitter on it before the paint dried, resulting in a very simple yet somehow magical angel. She held it out while it dried.

"What's that?"

The sweet voice caused Mist to turn her attention from the ornament to a small child who'd quite silently approached the table. Mist guessed the girl to be around five years old.

"It's an ornament," Mist said. "Something to hang on a Christmas tree or maybe in a window."

"My dad likes to hang things on the car mirror."

"I can picture that." Mist laughed.

"What's your name?" The child shuffled from one foot to the other several times and then turned in a circle.

"Mist."

"Mist?" the girl repeated.

"Mist. And what is your name?"

"Ashley."

"I haven't had the pleasure of meeting you before," Mist said. "Maybe you're visiting?"

Ashley nodded. "We're visiting my aunt Sallie. My mom's over there buying groceries." She waved a slender arm toward the grocery section of the store.

"Oh! You're Sally's niece," Mist said, putting it together now. The owner of Second Hand Sally's had mentioned family coming to visit.

"She's got a weird boyfriend," Ashley said with a dramatic sigh.

Mist, in spite of herself, burst out laughing. Indeed, Sallie and William Guthrie—better known as Wild Bill—had begun an unexpected courtship that had grown into a solid partnership.

"Well," Mist said, "I think sometimes 'weird' means 'different,' and that can be a good thing, right? Wouldn't it be boring if we were all the same?"

Ashley appeared to think that over before nodding. She then pointed at the gold angel ornament that still hung from Mist's fingers, now essentially dry. "That's pretty. I like the sparkles."

"Thank you. I like the sparkles too." Mist moved her arm

slightly, causing the angel to sway, the glitter catching in the light.

Ashley clapped her hands and looked at the stack of undecorated ornaments. "Are you going to make more?"

"I'm not," Mist said, noticing that Millie had returned and stood back, waiting to take over again. "But other people will make some to keep and some to give away."

"Oh."

"In fact..." Mist took a close look at the gold angel, feigning deep concentration. "I think I made this one to give away."

"Really?"

Mist tapped her lips with an index feature and then smiled. "Yes, that's right! I made this for you!"

Ashley's eyes grew wide. "For me?"

"Definitely. I think this angel wanted to be yours right from the start. That's why she wanted extra sparkles."

Ashley let Mist hand her the ornament, and Millie stepped up to add ribbon and wrap it in tissue paper. Ashley then ran around the table and threw herself in Mist's arms as a thank-you before taking the wrapped ornament and running off to find her mom.

"A thank-you hug," Millie said, taking a place behind the table as Mist stepped back out. "How precious. And that angel is beautiful."

"Indeed, she is." Mist smiled. "Just like the ornament that is going home with her."

Chapter Eight

Scarlet Brady was not at all what Mist expected, although she tried not to ever have expectations based simply on reservation phone calls. But this guest, who had sounded so bold and bright on the phone, so exuberant about coming to visit, seemed to have been replaced by a quiet, almost meek persona. The woman, a tall, slender figure with a single French braid, arrived in the late afternoon, silently filled out the registration, and retired to her room after politely thanking Mist for the key. She brought very little luggage, merely a small suitcase big enough for a few changes of clothes and miscellaneous items. Mist sensed a sadness about her, and she hoped spending the holidays with them would help.

"I'm a little worried about the last guest who checked in," Mist confessed to Betty as she tossed a mixed green salad to serve with the veggie chili.

"In what way?" Betty sliced freshly baked jalapeño cornbread into squares and arranged them on a large serving tray. Several whole peppers adorned the tray as garnish.

Mist thought about it before replying, trying to determine

just what seemed off. It wasn't so much that the guest seemed quiet. It was the fact her behavior was in sharp contrast to the person Mist had spoken with in the phone. "She's very subdued," Mist finally said. "I didn't sense any of the excitement she expressed when she made her reservation."

"How long ago did she make it?"

"Not too long ago. Maybe a month?"

"A lot can happen in a month," Betty said.

Mist nodded. "Yes, it can. Even in a day, even in a minute."

"Then again, maybe she's just not feeling well today," Betty mused.

"That's also possible," Mist said, though in her heart she felt it was something more. And she tended to trust her intuition.

"I'll take this cornbread out to the buffet," Betty said.

"Thank you. And I'm right behind you with the salad."

Dinner was a lively event with a mix of hotel guests and local townsfolk. Elise and Wesley Palmer, along with their daughter, Kylie, shared a table with the professor and Michael, much to Clive's delight at being able to teasingly call it a university faculty meeting.

Clara and Andrew sat with their friends Giulia and Tom, catching up on the months since they'd met in Tuscany.

Scarlet joined the others, just as Mist hoped. She sat next to Maisie at the largest table. Mist had slyly engaged Maisie to make sure Scarlet didn't sit alone, and Maisie made a point of gesturing Scarlet over when she appeared in the café doorway. In addition, Maisie's husband, Clayton—the town's fire chief—also sat with them as did their son, Clay Jr., and the baby, Cora. Sallie from the thrift shop and the semi-notorious Wild Bill filled other seats at the same table.

The meal was a success, which was to be expected at the

Moonglow Café. Tonight's gathering served the purpose of not only feeding people but also allowing them to get acquainted. After enjoying warm blueberry cobbler—vanilla bean ice cream was optional—guests moved to the front parlor, some stopping for cookies or glazed cinnamon nuts on their way through the lobby.

Clive crossed over to the fireplace and used a poker on the existing fire as the evening crowd settled in. Having analyzed it sufficiently, he added several new logs.

"Tell us about your trip to Tuscany," Michael said to Clara and Andrew as he took a seat in his favorite fireside chair. The professor chose a seat not far from there, and Clara, Andrew, Giulia, and Tom divided the plush couch in approximate quarters in order to sit together.

"Oh, it was marvelous!" Clara said. She clasped her hands together, eager to talk about it. "I'd never been to Italy, nor had Andrew." She gave her husband an affectionate smile, which he returned. "I'm so glad we chose Tuscany. And staying in Florence was perfect."

"Quite the lovely area," the professor said. "What was your favorite part of the trip?"

Clara responded immediately. "Such an impossible question! I could say the food or the art or the history or the architecture. Take your pick; they're all fabulous!"

"Everything we saw was so rich in culture," Andrew added. "And educational. I didn't know anything about art history, but after seeing Da Vinci's *Annunciation* at the Uffizi Gallery and then seeing Michelangelo's *David* at the Accademia Gallery, I wanted to know more. So I took a guided tour of the Duomo Complex."

"On his own," Clara added. "Not because I didn't want to see it but because there was a cooking class I wanted to take. And I was so glad I did, as it covered fabulous dishes we'd been enjoying at restaurants: *pappa al pomodoro, panzanella, gnocchi di ricotta,* and more."

"What a marvelous experience!" Elisa said. "How I would love to do that." She turned to Wes. "We should go sometime."

Wes agreed. "I'd love to attend an opera, maybe *La Traviata* or *Don Giovanni.*" He turned to Elisa and winked. "I'm sure you would too." Mist noticed the wink and found it intriguing.

"Yes, you must visit sometime, especially if you love opera," Giulia said. "You could see a performance in the Palazzo Pitti's courtyard or at Saint Mark's Anglican Church."

"Can I miss school?" Kylie asked with an impish grin that said she already knew the answer.

"We must get your contact information, Giulia," Elisa said.

"Absolutely." Giulia pulled out her cell phone, and the two women exchanged numbers.

"Can you teach me something in Italian?" Kylie asked.

Giulia nodded. "I'd be happy to. How about *Buon Natale?*"

Kylie attempted to repeat the phrase, catching on after several attempts.

"*Molto bene!*" Giulia said. "Very good. Now you know how to say Merry Christmas in Italian."

"*Buon Natale,*" Kylie repeated, looking very proud of herself.

"The Duomo Complex tour must have been fascinating, Andrew," the professor noted. "I believe Brunelleschi's dome is the largest brick dome in the world."

Andrew shrugged and grinned. "I believe you're correct. But if you want to know for sure, just ask the official guide from that tour!" He gestured to Tom.

"You kidnapped your tour guide and brought him back to the US with you?" Clive, eyebrows raised, looked impressed.

"And my wife," Tom added, patting Giulia's knee, "smuggled us right through customs."

Kylie flipped Andrew a thumbs-up.

"I rather suspect that isn't true," the professor said. "In spite of it being a brilliant story."

"It's true!" Andrew said. "I swear it!"

"Except..." Giulia nudged Tom.

"Well, except for the kidnapping and customs smuggling parts," Tom admitted. "Those are..."

"Creative embellishments," Clara said, laughing.

"But Tom does give those tours," Giulia explained, "and he gave the one the day Andrew was there. Then the two of them got talking afterward, and somehow we—all four of us—ended up having dinner together. We'd been thinking of coming to the US for the holidays, and when they told us about Timberton, it sounded perfect."

"So here we are," Tom said.

"And we're glad you're here," Mist said, first to Tom, then to the others. "I'm going to step out, but please help yourselves to the beverages and treats in the lobby. Betty and Clive will be available for anything else you might need."

After exchanging parting words, Mist made herself some peppermint tea in the kitchen and then retired to the small room in the back of the hotel that she kept for herself. Her easel awaited, along with small canvases, paints, and paintbrushes. It was time to begin preparing her traditional gifts for the guests.

Chapter Nine

Mist looked over the breakfast buffet, pleased with the assortment. The mushroom-and-cheese frittata, blueberry pancakes, bacon, and fresh fruit platter would be sure to get people off to a good start for the day. The following morning, being Christmas Eve, breakfast would be light in view of the extravagant dinner that would be served that night. But today was a chance to offer a pleasing morning meal to guests as well as any townsfolk who chose to come by. And there would be quite a few.

Clayton could always be counted on to show up for breakfast. Maisie, Clay Jr., and the new baby, Cora, might be with him, though he was also known to show up with a couple of firefighters from his crew. Mist smiled, knowing there was plenty of food. Those guys could certainly put down a meal, and for good reason: they worked hard.

Wild Bill and Sally were likely to show up too. Wild Bill still ran his greasy spoon down the road, the only option for food in Timberton aside from the Moonglow Café. But he had closed it for the holiday week.

Duffy wouldn't miss it or any meal, for that matter. Betty often teased Duffy that he'd set his store hours around the café's meal hours, opening just after the café closed in the morning and closing just before it opened in the evening. No one could blame him, of course. The Moonglow Café was much loved by the community. Duffy wasn't the only one with this reputation.

Clive was even more blatant in his intention to not miss meals, posting his gallery hours as "When Mist stops serving breakfast" to "When Mist starts serving dinner."

Those expected arrived, and the guests of the hotel joined them, delighting in the breakfast offerings and a chance to get to know each other more over coffee. Once appetites had been sufficiently satisfied, the café would transform itself for an annual tradition: Betty's cookie exchange.

With all the guests in-house already, Mist had been delighted that morning, pleased to see a soft snowfall and light breeze welcome the day. No one would be driving in winter weather when not used to it, and the view from every window in the hotel offered a picture-perfect winter scene. This included the front parlor, where the falling snow served as an enchanting backdrop to the old-fashioned Christmas tree. With a crackling fire that Clive had built before heading off to the gallery, many of the guests took advantage of the ambiance to settle into the parlor after breakfast to read or simply enjoy the fire.

Mist, getting a head start on the evening meal, prepped trays of lasagna so they'd be ready to pop in the oven in the late afternoon. Betty had insisted on doing this when the time came as well as making a large green salad to go with the dinner. Clive claimed the task of making garlic bread, and both Betty and Clive insisted they could handle making sure the meal was ready on time. Mist was grateful for their help. Although she still planned all the meals and cooked most of them, she'd had more offers of help—and accepted them without hesitation—since Rain was born.

Finished with food prep, she passed through the front parlor, pleased to see most of the hotel guests relaxing and visiting with each other.

Hollister, the deaf, nonspeaking, much-loved man who lived in a room on a lower level of the hotel not used for guests, had also come upstairs, and Mist was pleased to see him helping himself to a cup of coffee. The formerly homeless man, who had lived beneath the local railroad trestle for longer than anyone could say, had become a regular member of the hotel family, pitching in with tasks whenever needed. It had been wonderful to see him come out of his shell over the years.

Just behind Hollister was another member of the hotel family, this one with four paws. Hollister had found him abandoned outside the hotel two years before and adopted him after the little guy kept showing up at the back door. Due to his penchant for bacon—which Hollister had been "borrowing" from breakfast leftovers—he soon acquired the name Bacon. The friendly little brown pup had developed quite a fan base, and knowing this, he headed straight to the front parlor to greet people.

"Good morning, Bacon!" Clara said, remembering his sly arrival a previous holiday. She reached out and patted him on the head. Bacon continued around the room greeting people, eventually arriving in front of Scarlet.

"Well, hello there," Scarlet said, extending her arm as others had. But she stopped short of petting him, suddenly bursting into tears. This surprised herself as much as it did others. She managed a quick "excuse me" and abruptly headed out of the room, then out the front door. Mist, having observed this, followed. She found Scarlet on the front porch, dabbing her eyes with a tissue.

"I'm happy to listen if it will help," Mist offered as she stepped beside her. "Or I can allow you privacy. Whichever you prefer."

"Thank you," Scarlet said between sniffles. "I'm so sorry to make a scene in your lovely hotel. It's just… that dog reminds me so much of my Finley. He was such a sweet dog, the love of my life. I just lost him two weeks ago."

Mist reached out and touched the woman's shoulder. "I'm so sorry. That is a huge loss. Of course you're upset."

"Try telling that to a couple of my siblings," Scarlet said. "They say he was 'just a pet' and that I need to 'get a grip.'"

Mist shook her head. "He wasn't just a pet. He was a family member."

Scarlet sniffled again. "Yes, he was. And I can't believe he's gone. The house is so empty without him."

"Is there anything I can do to help?" Mist asked.

Scarlet shook her head. "I don't think so, though…" She trailed off, giving Mist the incentive to push a tiny bit.

"Though…" Mist nudged her to continue.

"Well, I could use an opinion. This might sound terrible, but I was thinking I might adopt another dog. But it's too soon, isn't it? Wouldn't it be like I was replacing him?"

"Only you can answer those questions," Mist said.

"But what do you think?"

Mist chose her words carefully. "I don't think one pet replaces another, just as one person doesn't replace another. Each person or pet is unique and important."

"Finley always hated it when I was sad," Scarlet said, her voice shaky. "He'd snuggle up to me, try to comfort me."

"Animals are very sensitive," Mist said. "And very perceptive. Perhaps more than people sometimes. I don't think he would want you to be sad."

"Yes, you're probably right," Scarlet said. "Looks like I have some things to think about." She wrapped her arms around herself and shivered. "It's a little chilly. I didn't even think about that when I hurried out here without a jacket."

Mist laughed. "It is winter after all. How about some hot chocolate or hot apple cider to warm you back up?" She gestured to the front door.

"Sounds perfect."

Chapter Ten

Mist curled one arm around Rain in the baby wrap as she circled tables that had been pulled together in one long row. With her free arm, she arranged quilted placemats from one end to the other, varied fabric prints offering a kaleidoscope of designs. Maisie had surprised her by dropping off a floral centerpiece of red and white parrot tulips to go in the center of the table. The ruffled texture of the flowers added a whimsical touch.

Most of this festive display would soon be covered with delectable treats from those participating in Betty's annual cookie exchange. The event was a long-standing tradition in Timberton, dating back before Mist arrived in the small town. Betty had always felt that sweet treats would bring people together for holiday cheer and camaraderie, not to mention a bit of intriguing gossip. And the popularity of the event year after year proved that it was so.

Although Mist always let Betty run the event—after all, it was her pride and joy—she enjoyed helping her prepare for it. This included presentation details like this year's quilted placemats as well as containers for participants to fill with consolidated goodies to take home with them at the end. This year, she'd come across a collection of vintage cookie tins at an antique shop in Missoula. The tins were roughly the same size with different images on the edges—ice skaters at an outdoor rink, a red sleigh passing through a winter forest, and a group of children building a sweet family of snowmen. All offered a glimpse of nostalgia and served the purpose of gathering cookies and other treats perfectly. Townsfolk who attended the exchange would have a keepsake that they could use again.

Michael had set up music, choosing upbeat holiday classics to play throughout the event. Songs like "Santa Claus is Coming to Town," "Frosty the Snowman," and "Jingle Bell Rock" were sure to set the mood, providing a cheerful background to the festivities.

"Oh, it looks wonderful!" Betty exclaimed as she arrived in the café and looked over the table display. "And I can't wait to see the goodies everyone brings this year." Her outfit matched the festive spirit of the event. She'd paired a not-at-all-ugly "ugly sweater" featuring dancing candy canes to match her red slacks and white bangles. The white touches picked up the soft gray of her hair. The overall effect was charming.

"It's always fun to see what cookies show up," Mist agreed. "And other treats." Apparently Rain agreed as well, at least that's what Mist and Betty decided a perfectly timed though unintelligible exclamation from her meant.

"I know Sallie is bringing gingerbread sandwich cookies," Betty said. "She was talking about them at Duffy's the other day."

"Perfect for the season," Mist noted.

"And Marge will be dropping off fudge from her shop," Betty said. "She says this variety is her cousin Josie's favorite. So she calls it Josie's Fudge."

"And just how did you find this out?" Mist smiled, already knowing the answer. Betty always kept a steady supply of her favorite addiction around.

"I happened to stop in for a few more caramels. But you knew that."

"I did."

The front door opened and closed, and Maisie—Cora in tow—entered the café. "Let me help! I need to help! Give me a task! Anything, it doesn't matter!"

Betty grinned. "Clayton's parents driving you crazy?"

"How did you guess?" Maisie brought Cora over to greet Rain, which was always entertaining to see, generally a display of gurgles and arm waving.

"Well, let me see." Betty pretended to think hard before answering. "Busy season, new baby, a six-year-old, your flower business, and in-laws staying with you for the holidays. It's not really a stretch."

Maisie sighed. "You're right. And it's a joyful stretch. I wouldn't change a thing. But sometimes I just need to get out for a few minutes. And I wanted a little time with just Cora. Her grandparents are enthralled with her, of course, but they'll get by without doting over her for fifteen minutes. Your cookie exchange was the perfect excuse for a quick escape."

"Everything seems ready," Mist said, "including those lovely parrot tulips you sent over."

"Aren't they fun?" Maisie looked at the effect they created. "They have such a party feeling to them."

"And that's exactly what the cookie exchange is," Betty said. "Oh, how I look forward to this every year. And Clive looks forward to the cookies, of course."

"So does Clayton," Maisie said. "I'm under orders to bring some home. So what can I do to help?"

"We can greet people out in the lobby," Mist suggested.

"With the girls." Maisie agreed, and the four of them—adults and babies—took positions in the lobby just as the first attendee arrived.

"Look at you two and your darling girls!" Millie exclaimed as she entered. She brushed a few snowflakes off her hair, set a large, covered plate down on the registration desk, and hung her coat up. "Crème brûlée cookies," she announced as she picked the plate up and lifted the covering off.

"Those look delicious!" Maisie exclaimed.

"You get first choice of a spot on the table," Mist said. "Just pick whatever quilted print you like."

Millie moved into the café, where Betty greeted her as she set the cookies down. Sally and Glenda showed up next with orange crisps and snowball cookies. Others followed not far behind, and soon the festive table was filled with peanut butter muffin cookies, lemon bars, old-fashioned molasses cookies, Christmas bark, walnut butter cookies, and more. As promised, Marge showed up with Josie's Fudge. After another dozen townsfolk showed up with various sweets, the table looked like something from a sugar-laden fantasy. The vintage tins were a hit, and soon they boasted fabulous assortments of sweet treats.

"Betty loves this," Maisie noted as she and Mist observed the gathering from the front lobby. "She's absolutely beaming."

"Yes, she is." Mist smiled as she watched the hotelkeeper move about the room, exchanging pleasantries—and undoubtedly a bit of gossip—and admiring the choices of sweets that participants had chosen for their assortments. "She looks forward to this every year."

Maisie turned to Mist. "And what do you look forward to? What's your favorite part of the holiday festivities? I bet it's a hard question to answer."

"Not at all. That's an easy to question to answer," Mist said as she watched a guest debate between a peppermint brownie and a raspberry bar. The solution was obvious. She took one of each.

Maisie's eyebrows lifted. "Really? With everything that goes on here, you can name something as your favorite?"

"Of course, Maisie, and I'm sure you already know the answer."

"What is it then?"

Mist smiled. "It's everything."

Chapter Eleven

With the cookie exchange wrapping up and a little more than two hours left before dinner, Mist took advantage of the time to pay a visit to Clive's gallery. She always enjoyed seeing the art and jewelry on display, but she also had an ulterior motive for stopping by this time—to check on a gift Clive had been designing for her to give to Michael. Conveniently, Michael had offered to watch Rain for a bit, promising Dickens this time around.

Mist had seen the initial sketch of the gift, but now it was ready, and she was eager to see it. Clive had insisted on keeping it in his possession until Christmas Eve, which struck Mist as a little odd, but he'd insisted he'd need to do a last-minute touch-up to make the surprise perfect. However, he encouraged her to come see it, which is exactly what she planned to do now.

The gallery was busy, just as Mist knew it would be. With only two days left before Christmas, people were in buying mode, and some of the smaller pieces Clive carried fit the needs of many. Although his custom jewelry included some high-dollar designs, smaller charms and other trinkets made for affordable gifts. Especially popular were silver Christmas ornaments in varying holiday designs: snowmen, wreaths, stockings, candy canes, and more. These had started out as a special gift he made each year for Betty but now were available to customers.

Mist sauntered through the gallery, admiring paintings from other local artists and pausing to see her own. The four-by-four miniatures were displayed in a quilt-like pattern on the wall with a slight space between each one. These fell into the affordable category of gifts, as Mist was firm about keeping the prices low. She didn't make them as a source of income; she made them to give others the gift of art, of an image created by brushstrokes, much the way she saw people's lives created. When asked about this, she would calmly note that life is full of paint and paintbrushes. It's just a matter of choosing what to do with those.

"I could never paint," a woman admiring the miniature paintings said. "I can barely draw a stick figure."

Mist observed the woman, estimating her to be in her forties. She had a kind face, a pleasant smile, and eyes that sparkled when she spoke.

"Perhaps you paint with something else," Mist suggested. "You might paint with words or with music. Or perhaps with your time."

"Oh! I never thought of it like that. Thank you."

Mist brushed the woman's arm gently as she moved on, whispering a few final words. "It doesn't matter what you paint with. Just paint your life."

Clive was at the register, ringing up a sale for a tall gentleman with silver hair. He placed a gift box in a handle bag and thanked the customer.

"No, thank *you*," the man said before turning away. "My wife loves gingerbread houses. They remind her of her childhood. She's going to be thrilled with this gingerbread house charm."

"Another happy customer," Mist said as she approached Clive. "Those charms are adorable."

"They're selling really well," Clive admitted.

"I'm not surprised," Mist said. "It's a sweet gift, something nostalgic, and this is a nostalgic time of year for many."

"I bet you're here to see this." Clive pulled a small box out from beneath the register and opened it.

"It's perfect!" Mist clasped her hands in front of her chest. "Thank you, Clive. He's going to love it."

Clive looked pleased. "He will. I'm sure of it." He closed the box and slipped it back under the register.

Mist looked past Clive to a desk in back where a young woman was adding gold ribbon to a small jewelry box.

"That must be Addison, your new part-timer."

"Yes." Clive looked around toward the desk. "She's great. I don't know what I would have done without her this season. I hope she'll stay during the year. I'd love more time to help Betty around the hotel. And Addison lives here now, just moved here a few weeks ago. She loves your miniature paintings."

"How wonderful," Mist said. "I think I'll go introduce myself."

Addison looked up as Mist approached. "May I help you?" She offered a friendly smile that was neither off-putting nor sales aggressive. Mist liked her immediately. She fit right in with the gallery's casual ambiance.

"I just thought I'd introduce myself. I'm Mist, and I believe you're Addison?" Although a statement, Mist's inflection was that of a question, designed to allow the girl a quick answer.

"Oh, you're Mist!" Addison beamed. "I'm so glad to meet you. I love your paintings. I plan to buy one or two for my new place. I just moved here."

"Yes, Clive told me. Welcome to Timberton. I think you'll love it here."

"I already do," Addison said. "It's such a peaceful town, and the people here are so friendly. Your librarian already set me up with a library card, and the owner of the grocery store offered to build me a bookcase."

"Yes, Millie is a gem. She'll have great reading recommendations. And Duffy is a magician with wood."

Addison looked up toward the front of the store. "Excuse me a moment while I deliver these." She headed up to meet Clive at the register, a small stack of wrapped gift boxes in her hands.

Mist looked around the back of the gallery while Addison was up front, suddenly noticing that she and Addison hadn't been entirely alone. Curled up on a soft blanket behind the desk was a medium-sized dog with black-and-tan fur forming a patchwork design not unlike a dark version of a calico cat. When the dog spotted Mist, he greeted her with a wagging tail and an expression that would have to be called a smile.

"Well, hello there!" Mist leaned down and extended a hand, allowing the dog to decide whether to greet her or not. It immediately did, offering an affectionate lick of Mist's hand. Mist returned it with a few scrunches behind the dog's ear.

"I see you met Lily," Addison said as she returned.

"Yes." Mist stood up. "Your dog is beautiful and so sweet."

Addison nodded, looking down at the sweet ball of fur. "Thank you, but she's not actually my dog. I'm fostering her until she can find a home. Her owner passed away, and no one in her family could take her."

"Really?" Mist leaned down to pet the dog again. "Well, she's lucky to have such a nice foster home. Thank you for offering her a safe place for now."

"She's so sweet," Addison said. "If I didn't have a cat who

strongly opposes the very existence of dogs, I would adopt her myself."

Mist laughed. "A cat with a catitude."

"Exactly!"

"I'll leave you to your work," Mist said. "Try to come by the hotel tomorrow afternoon. I believe Clive closes early. You can have some hot chocolate and enjoy the decorations and treats. Feel free to bring Lily too."

"She's welcome at the hotel?" Addison's expression lit up.

"Absolutely!" Mist said. "All are welcome. And it might be that dogs are especially welcome this year."

Chapter Twelve

"That salad looks wonderful!" Mist exclaimed as she entered the kitchen through the side door after returning from the gallery.

"It does look appetizing, if I do say so myself." Betty grinned as she tossed the giant bowl of greens. Remnants of cucumber, tomato, avocado, apple, dried cranberries, and sliced almonds littered the counter. "This should be delicious with your vinaigrette, Mist."

"It seems you have another salad right there on the counter," Mist said.

"Very funny." Betty covered the bowl with plastic wrap. "I'll put this in the downstairs fridge since the one up here seems to be a lasagna warehouse." She chuckled.

"Not for long," Mist said. "In about three minutes, this one will be all yours." Mist peeked into the fridge and pulled out large trays of lasagna. She set the oven to preheat and gestured to the fridge. "It's all yours, Betty. Just a few loaves of garlic bread on the bottom, but the other shelves are all yours."

"Excellent," Betty said as she slid the salad bowl on the top shelf. "It just barely fits with room below it for a smaller bowl of onions. I know not everyone likes onions, so I didn't mix them in."

"Smart," Mist said, approving. "It's always nice to give people choices."

"You might want to go check out the front parlor," Betty said. "It's quite a lively scene. I can put the lasagna in the oven when it's preheated."

"I think I'll do that. Thank you, Betty. It's time I give Michael a break from Rain anyway."

The sounds of cheerful activity reached Mist as soon as she stepped out of the kitchen and into the café, and they only grew in volume as she approached the front parlor. She was pleased to see all the in-house guests in one portion of the parlor or another. Giulia and Tom were admiring the ornaments on the Christmas tree. Andrew and the professor were focused on their yearly chess game. Clara worked a jigsaw puzzle on a back table, and Elisa and Wes manned the piano, Elisa providing percussive accents by tapping the top of the piano with her hands while Wes played Christmas tunes. Kylie was sprawled on the floor, giving Bacon affectionate pats on the head while engaged in what Mist was certain to be a one-sided discussion.

Michael looked up and smiled as Mist approached, and she felt her heart flutter at the sight of him holding Rain. He was a wonderful, devoted father, just as she knew he'd be. Seeing them together gave her joy all over again.

"Ah, the traditional Christmas story," Mist said, spying a copy of *A Christmas Carol* next to Michael.

"She loves the voices that go with the ghosts," Michael said.

"She loves the narrator," Mist said, smiling. "As do I." She kissed Michael on his forehead and lifted Rain from his lap. Rain made cooing noises and reached for Mist's ear. She'd learned early on not to wear earrings, especially with her habit of wearing styles with dangling shells or feathers. True to what she'd been told by Maisie, Rain had become enchanted with reaching out and grasping whatever she could reach.

Tom moved away from the tree and took to watching Andrew and the professor's chess game. From the expression on his face, Mist was certain he wanted to offer input but knew better than to do so.

Mist approached the tree and stood near Giulia, who was admiring one of the silver ornaments that Clive had given Betty over the years. Giulia smiled as she saw Mist approach, yet Mist was certain she also took a step back. To anyone else, it might have seemed she was making room for Mist by the tree, although no one else was there at the moment. But Mist had a feeling it was something else.

"This is a charming ornament," Giulia said as she held up a silver cluster of three candles before moving on to ornaments of similar designs. "So is that one, and that one. And the sapphires make them so special. I've never seen ornaments exactly like that."

"Clive designs them," Mist said. "And those are Yogo sapphires, which are unique to this area."

"They're beautiful." Giulia replaced the ornament she'd been holding and turned toward Mist, taking a cautious look at Rain.

"Would you like to hold her?" Mist asked, almost certain of the reaction she'd get, and she was right.

"Oh no!" Giulia said, realizing immediately that she'd answered too quickly. "I mean thank you. She's beautiful. I'm just not... I mean... I wouldn't want to hurt her. She looks so fragile."

"They're not as fragile as they seem." Mist took a soft ladybug ornament off the tree and gave it to Rain, who instantly put it in her mouth. "You know, when I was first expecting, I was terrified."

"Really?" Giulia looked at Mist, eyes wide. "You don't seem like someone who could be terrified of anything."

Mist smiled. "In general, I'm not. Moving here to Timberton, running the café, creating art, welcoming guests, even getting married two years ago. None of that scared me."

"But…" Giulia fiddled with a random ornament on the tree as Mist continued.

"But bringing a human being into the world? That's a whole new level of the unknown, especially with a first child."

"I see." Giulia looked at Rain as if expecting the child to give her an answer to a question that had yet to be asked. "All that responsibility, so many decisions to make, so many ways to get it wrong."

"You'll be fine," Mist said, her voice soft, almost a whisper.

"I'll be…?" Giulia turned toward Mist, questioning.

"When are you due?"

Giulia sighed. "June. I just found out."

Mist nodded. "I found out at Christmas too. Couldn't handle garlic."

Giulia laughed. "Cheese here! And I teach Italian-cooking classes!"

"You may have to adjust some of your menus!" Mist joined Giulia in laughter just as Tom walked up.

"What's with you two?"

"Girl talk," Mist said.

"And baby talk," Giulia added. She reached out for the first time and let Rain wrap her fingers around one of her own.

Tom smiled. "Ah, you told her."

"Actually, she guessed," Giulia said. She and Mist exchanged smiles.

"We're very excited," Tom said. "It's just taking some time

to sink in." He put his arm around Giulia's shoulders and joined her in playing with Rain.

Mist looked from one face to the other, seeing clearly that the joy outweighed the fear. She felt some of that joy run through her, not only for her own gift of Rain, but for a young Italian baby-to-be who would have devoted parents and a life yet to be discovered.

Chapter Thirteen

"*Delizioso!*" Tom exclaimed as he aimed his fork at a second bite of lasagna.

"*Squisito,*" Giulia said, backing him up.

"*Buon Natale!*" Kylie chirped, causing Giulia to laugh.

"Mist, maybe you need to come back to Tuscany with us and teach the cooking classes for me," Giulia suggested.

Clive cleared his throat. "Oh, no you don't. You're not stealing her away from here. We'd be stuck with Wild Bill's cooking." He turned to Bill quickly. "No offense, Bill."

"None taken, Clive. I wouldn't eat my own cooking either!" This resulted in a round of laughter as others agreed.

"He's not even allowed in the kitchen when I'm around," Sallie said as she patted his shoulder affectionately.

"Wes does most of the cooking for us," Elisa said.

"And I help," Kylie said. "Especially with bread or muffins or cookies."

"It's true," Wes said. "She's quite the baker."

"That's a talent right there, you know," Giulia said,

directing her comment to Kylie. "Good bakers are very in demand."

"Really?" Kylie regarded Giulia.

"Absolutely."

Mist smiled as she listened to the discussion. She was pleased to see a young girl of Kylie's age fascinated with cooking, baking in particular.

"Maybe someday in the future," Giulia suggested, "you might come to Tuscany and learn some baking tricks."

"Way, way in the future," Elisa said, laughing. "Though... it would be lovely to visit." She looked at Wes, who looked agreeable.

Dinner conversation continued as guests exchanged tidbits about their lives as well as holiday sentiments and thoughts about the coming new year. Finally, lured by a sizable tray of cookies, the group moved into the front parlor.

Upbeat renditions of classic Christmas carols flowed through the room as guests took seats or chose to stand by the tree or near the fireplace. Andrew and the professor headed to the chess board. Betty and Mist encouraged people to help themselves to hot chocolate, hot mulled cider, or hot mulled wine to go with the cookies. A pitcher of ice water stood by for those not looking for a hot beverage. And a bit of brandy had been known to mysteriously appear with just the right sly request.

"Look at that angel on the tree," Kylie said, admiring one particular ornament. "It's like the ones down at that store with the soda fountain."

"Yes, it is," Mist said. "I made that one down at Duffy's, the store you're thinking of. Did you get a chance to make one yet?"

Kylie shook her head. "No. But I want to."

"We could go tomorrow if he's open," Elisa said. "I wouldn't mind making one too."

"I'm sure he'll be open," Mist said. "At least for half the day. People still need to buy things on Christmas Eve."

"Or they might need an ice-cream soda," Kylie said. "An angel *and* an ice-cream soda."

"Yes, that's a possibility." Mist smiled as she exchanged looks with Elisa. The angel project Mist could vouch for, but permission for an ice-cream soda fell to the mother.

"What do you say we go around lunchtime?" Elisa suggested.

"Deal." Kylie rubbed her hands together, pleased with the plan.

"Where are we going around lunchtime?" Wes asked, having overheard the last part of the conversation. "Am I invited?"

"We're going to that store with the soda fountain," Kylie said. "To make an angel ornament like that one on the tree."

"Actually, you'll want to make two," Mist said. "That's the secret of this project. One you keep, and one you give away."

"Something to think about between now and tomorrow," Elisa said as she and Wes moved to the sofa near the fireplace while Kylie occupied herself by checking out other ornaments on the tree.

"I've always been fond of angels," Clara said. "I used to love watching *Touched by an Angel*. Roma Downey and Della Reese were perfect together."

"It was *Highway to Heaven* for me," Scarlet said. "I adored Michael Landon."

"Well, if we're going to talk about shows with angels, don't forget movies," Elisa pointed out. "Like that clever angel played by Cary Grant in *The Bishop's Wife*. He had a mischievous streak!"

"You can't leave this one out," Wes said. "What about the guardian angel who showed George Bailey—that was Jimmy

Stewart, of course— that life was worth living in *It's a Wonderful Life?*"

"Oh yes," Giulia said. "Clarence, the angel, played by Henry Travers. He was wonderful!"

"What about that one with Fred MacMurray," Clara said. "*Charley and the Angel.* It had Harry Morgan as the angel. And Cloris Leachman was in it, along with Kurt Russell."

"A very young Kurt Russell," Elisa pointed out. "That movie is from the '70s."

"Angels are well represented in multiple mediums," Tom added. "Take art. There's a beautiful *Musician Angel* painting by Melozzo da Forlì in the Vatican Pinacoteca—the art gallery. We've been fortunate to see it."

Giulia picked up from there. "And if you go to Dresden—which we haven't, unfortunately, but we want to—you can see Raphael's *Two Cherubs*, which is a detail from the *Sistine Madonna.*"

"I know that one," Elise said. "The two little angels?"

Giulia nodded. "It's very famous, that section of the painting with the cherubs. Not everyone knows those are part of a larger piece."

Mist gestured toward an area at the rear of the room. "The jigsaw puzzle on that back table is of that very painting."

"Yes," Clara said. "I was working on that earlier."

"I want to see." Kylie jumped up and walked to the table. She picked up the box to see the picture. "It's so pretty! I want to do this."

"I'll help," Scarlet said, walking over to join Kylie. "I love jigsaw puzzles. They're so relaxing."

"It's crossword puzzles for me," Giulia said. "I never get tired of them."

"In Italian or in English?" Clara asked.

"Both. It helps me keep up with both languages. Word games are great for that."

Mist adjusted the music to softer jazz arrangements and took a look around the room, her heart warmed by what she saw. Guests who had been strangers only a day before now came together as friends, sharing experiences, sharing hobbies, and simply sharing the joy of being together. It was everything she hoped for each holiday season and everything that came to pass. To her delight, she knew this year would be no different.

Chapter Fourteen

"What an absolutely gorgeous day out there!" Clara observed as she looked out the front window of the café. She'd been one of the first guests up that morning. She and Andrew now sat at a center table, enjoying fresh melon slices and cinnamon scones from the casual morning buffet. Like everyone, they planned to save their appetites for the Christmas Eve feast later.

"These scones are delicious," Andrew said.

"Thank you, Andrew," Mist said. "But I can't take all the credit. I had an excellent helper."

"Me! *Buon Natale!*" Kylie popped out of the kitchen, looking every bit the young baker with her hair pulled back and flour-covered apron that hung a little lower than it did when Betty wore it.

"They're perfect, Kylie," Clara said. "What a great start to the day. Delicious scones and lovely weather."

"You should bundle up and take a walk," Betty suggested. "The snow is going to start up again later, but that sunshine now is lovely."

Andrew turned to Clara. "An excellent suggestion. What do you think?"

"It sounds wonderful," Clara agreed. "Maybe we can do some window shopping and also check out the town park."

"Now that you mention it, walking around the park is a great idea," Betty said. "Marge at the candy shop was just talking about snowmen—or *snowpeople*, I suppose—that visitors were building there."

"A contest?" Clara asked. "I think we built snowmen there a few years ago."

Betty shook her head. "No, it's nothing official. People just get creative."

"The park is a gathering place," Mist said as she added warm scones to the buffet. "Activities happen spontaneously. You two might even find yourselves joining in."

"That sounds like a good way to spend Christmas Eve day," Andrew said. "I'm all in favor of a walk around town."

Elisa and Wes entered the café and joined Clara and Andrew. Scarlet, Giulia, and Tom followed shortly behind. They stopped at the buffet and then took seats at various tables.

"Delicious scones!" Elisa said upon taking a bite. She looked at Kylie and smiled with pride.

Wes's ears perked up as he recognized a recording of "Wassail, Wassail" flowing from the sound system.

"Mannheim Steamroller," Wes piped up. "Great choice."

"I do like them," Elisa said, "but I confess to being partial to Pentatonix."

"Because you love their harmonies," Wes pointed out.

"Very true," Elisa said. "There's something peaceful about good harmonies. They're soothing, calming."

Clara spoke up. "Just give me the old crooners and I'm happy," she said. "Bing Crosby singing 'Winter Wonderland' or Frank Sinatra singing 'White Christmas.'"

"Or Perry Como singing 'Do You Hear What I Hear?'" Betty added.

"Or Nat King Cole singing 'The Christmas Song,'" Elisa added, singing the first line. "Chestnuts roasting on..." Wes picked up the next line, and the two sang a verse.

"What do you sing at Christmas in Italy?" Kylie asked Giulia.

"We sing many of the same songs. We also have '*Tu Scendi dalla Strelle*,' which is very popular," Giulia said. "In English that would be 'from starry skies descending' or 'you come down from the stars.'"

"Yes!" Elisa exclaimed. "I know that one. Andrea Bocelli does a beautiful rendition of that."

"Indeed." Giulia grinned. "No one would argue with that."

Andrew looked around. "Where's Nigel? Morning is not quite the same if I can't give him a hard time about something."

Betty laughed. "He went down to Duffy's to make an angel ornament to send to his niece in London. And Clive is already down at the gallery. There'll be people looking for last-minute gifts."

"We'll stop at both places when we head out on the town," Clara said. She turned to Scarlet. "It's a nice day to get out."

Scarlet looked out the window. "You're right. I think I'm going to read in the front parlor for a while. But I'll step out later."

"There's a nice fire going in there," Mist said. "And Michael is home with Rain, so you can have his favorite chair by the fireplace." She lowered her voice. "Not that it's his chair, but we don't tell him that."

"Sounds perfect. I think I'll take my coffee in and claim that chair as mine for now." Smiling, Scarlet thanked Mist for the melon and scones and moved to the front parlor.

Kylie stood up and pushed her chair in. "I'm going to copy Mist's scone recipe and then go make another angel ornament."

"That sounds like a great plan," Elisa said. "Come get us when you're ready to go."

"Why don't I walk her down there?" Mist offered. "I'm sure I'll need something from his store. Then you two can relax in the front parlor."

"That would be very nice," Elisa said. "Thank you."

Kylie frowned momentarily. "I don't really need…" Her voice trailed off at the look on her mother's face. "Okay. I get it, I get it."

"This town is actually very safe," Mist said to Kylie though making sure Elisa and Wes could hear. "And Duffy's is just down the block. But we want your parents to be comfortable and not worry on their vacation, right?"

"Right. Now can we copy the recipe?"

Mist smiled. "Let's go."

One by one and two by two, guests headed off in different directions as discussed, some going out, some staying in. Scarlet took the seat unofficially known as Michael's, understanding immediately why he rarely sat elsewhere. The chair was the perfect combination of plush softness and support. It was the kind that could easily put someone to sleep, especially by the warmth of the fire. Giulia and Tom also came in to enjoy the fire, settling on the couch. And Elisa and Wes picked out books from the parlor's bookshelf and chose places in the room to read.

The soothing sound of holiday music combined with the comfortable chair and fire only allowed Scarlet a chapter or two before her eyes began to close. She fell into a light sleep, waking again when she heard voices in the front lobby.

"Addison! I'm glad you stopped by!" Betty said.

"I was intrigued by Mist's suggestion of hot chocolate and

treats, but I'm also delivering this." The sound of paper rustling followed. "Clive said to hide it in the back of the tree somewhere."

Betty headed for the Christmas tree, followed by Addison, who stopped under the archway, Lily by her side.

"What a sweet dog!" Elisa exclaimed. "Is she yours?"

"Just for now," Addison said. "I'm fostering her until she finds a home."

Lily came over to Elisa and accepted a pat on the head. She then circled the room, accepting the same from others, always moving on to the next person.

"She knows how to work a room!" Giulia noted, laughing.

"Yes, she does," Addison said. "She's really the sweetest dog."

When Lily got to Scarlet, she accepted a pat on the head and then, to everyone's surprise, Scarlet included, sat down next to her, rested her head against Scarlet's knee, and then curled up by her feet.

"Oh my!" Scarlet's hand flew to her mouth, and then she tentatively reached down to pet Lily.

"She really likes you," Elisa said.

Addison nodded. "Yes, she does."

Scarlet looked up, tears in her eyes. "I know, I can tell. But..." She sat back up after patting Lily one more time. "I don't think I'm ready."

"You just lost one," Addison guessed.

"Yes." Scarlet nodded. "My Finley, only two weeks ago. He was my best friend."

"I'm so sorry," Addison said. "That's very hard." She pulled a pen and paper from her jacket pocket and scribbled her contact information. "In case you want to visit her while you're here," she said as she handed it to Scarlet. "She never gets tired of taking walks."

"Well," Elisa said after Addison and Lily left, "I think a walk sounds like a good idea right now. Maybe I can preemptively work off the calories that I'm bound to take in a few hours from now." She stood up, and Giulia joined her.

"An excellent idea," Giulia said. "I understand Christmas Eve dinner here is a gourmet feast."

Tom looked at Wes and nodded to the chess board. "Shall we give it a try while Andrew and the professor are away?"

"Why not?" Wes agreed, and the two took places at the table.

"Feel like joining us, Scarlet?" Giulia asked.

Scarlet smiled but shook her head. "I think I'll keep reading. It's very cozy here by the fire. You two enjoy your walk." And with Giulia and Elisa on their way out, and Tom and Wes arranging chess pieces on the board, Scarlet stared into the fire for a few minutes and then returned to her book.

Chapter Fifteen

MIST CIRCLED THE CAFÉ, LIGHTING VOTIVE CANDLES THAT she'd placed in the middle of the floral centerpieces. One by one, each table began to glow in the near dark, giving the room a magical ambiance. The lighting would come up before guests entered. But for these moments, when Mist allowed herself solitude, she only needed to maneuver her way around the tables. Tiny white lights draped from the ceiling were enough to allow her to do so.

To say she did this in solitude was not entirely true this year, though her companion remained respectfully silent while Mist took in the room as if she knew this time was important.

Mist picked Rain up from the baby chair and held her gently. She had made mother-daughter outfits for the special occasion by cutting off the bottom foot and a half of a long, flowing ivory gown with a pale leaf print, creating a matching dress for Rain. Mist wore a rhinestone barrette with hers and made a soft fabric green bow for Rain. Together they looked like they'd just stepped out of a Christmas forest.

Satisfied that all was ready, she stood back, pleased.

Although each meal served in the café was special, the Christmas Eve dinner was the most special of all. And now the elegant tables, the upscale buffet setting, and the duo of chairs at one end of the room, a guitar beside each one, stood waiting for the evening celebration dinner to begin.

As arranged in advance, she opened the kitchen door first, where Elisa and Wes were waiting to take their places with guitars. Just behind them, Betty and Maisie brought out the hot dishes for the buffet. As the musicians began to serenade the room with soothing acoustic guitar music, Mist opened the café doors to an enthusiastic—and hungry—crowd.

In keeping with the elegance of the holiday dinner, guests and townsfolk had donned their fancier clothes. Michael wore a tailored shirt and gray-green vest that picked up the color of his eyes, which Mist always referred to as patina. And the professor sported a dinner jacket with an especially elegant bow tie.

Even Wild Bill showed up in upscale attire, which few had even suspected he owned. Elisa and Kylie wore similar—though *not* identical upon Kylie's insistence—dresses and sweaters. The room was soon filled with fabrics and flair not seen at other times of the year—velvet and satin, rhinestones and ribbons.

Clayton, his visiting parents, and both children—Clay Jr. and Cora, celebrating her first Christmas—took seats at a large table, saving a place for Maisie to settle into after all the food was served. Other townsfolk filled in additional seats at the table for twelve. Wild Bill and Sally arrived together, as was now expected, and were soon joined by Clara and Andrew. Scarlet arrived with Kylie, arranged so the "eleventeen" young lady would not have to enter alone while her parents played. Scarlet let Kylie choose a table, where they kept two seats ready for Elisa and Wes to slide into once they finished the musical accompaniment. Giulia and Tom also joined that table.

Christmas Eve dinner at the Timberton Hotel was always a highlight of the season and, as such, was well attended. Townsfolk arrived dressed in holiday attire, lining up at the buffet for the exquisite meal. Millie, Marge, and Glenda showed up together, taking a well-deserved break from their library, candy shop, and beauty salon businesses. Clayton's fire crew was never known to miss the meal, and even Ernie from the local watering hole, Pop's Parlor, closed his place for the night in order to enjoy the feast. Duffy, of course, was there along with many others from the town. All chatted with each other as they went down the buffet line and piled their plates high with roast turkey with cranberry-apple stuffing, Parmesan herb-roasted acorn squash, and other delicious selections.

Giulia glanced at Mist as she and Tom served themselves balsamic-glazed salmon and rice pilaf. "Did you know it's a tradition in Italy to have seafood on Christmas Eve?" she asked. Mist attempted a noncommittal shrug of her shoulders, though her smile was enough to make Giulia suspect the truth. The salmon had been an addition to the menu after the Italian couple made their reservations.

"Did you make it to Duffy's today?" Mist asked Elisa and Kylie as she refilled the water glasses at their table. "You mentioned wanting to go there." Elisa and Wes had set their guitars aside to join everyone for the meal, just as Mist had insisted when they offered to play.

"Oh yes," Elisa said. "All three of us went." She indicated Kylie and Scarlet.

"We all made angel ornaments," Scarlet said. "I'm giving my second one to a neighbor who's essentially housebound. Such a sweet lady. She lives alone."

"I'm sure she'll love it," Mist said.

"Mine is for my teacher," Kylie announced. "She's sort of weird but also sort of nice. Like, *nice* weird, you know?"

Scarlet fought back a laugh. "Yes, I believe I do."

Mist nodded, thinking Kylie's character description of "nice weird" was a decent portrayal of a personality. She'd known a few "nice weird" people in her life, all of them lovely.

"My angel ornament is going overseas," Elisa said, "to a cousin who's in the military. He was nervous about being deployed, so I hope he sees the ornament as a guardian angel."

"They will all love them," Mist said. "Sometimes a small gift offers more comfort than we might expect."

After continuing around the room to make sure everyone was content, Mist slid into the chair beside Michael, allowing herself to exhale and finally relax.

"Lovely dinner as always, Mist," Michael said. He then turned to Rain. "Isn't that right?"

Mist caressed the baby's head. "I do think she's enjoying her first Christmas Eve dinner."

The professor cleared his throat, having overheard from a neighboring table. "I dare say she *should* be with the special treatment she's getting," he quipped. "I didn't get any home-made apple puree."

"I could remedy that if you'd like," Mist offered, holding up a spoonful as if redirecting it from Rain to Wild Bill.

The professor let out an exaggerated sigh. "That's quite okay. I'll have to make do with my roast turkey and glazed salmon and that portobello mushroom wellington. And pecan pie, of course."

"Somehow no one's feeling sorry for you, Nigel," Andrew pointed out. "Maybe Mist could give you apple puree for your Christmas breakfast instead."

"She wouldn't dare," the professor proclaimed.

"I wouldn't put it past her, Nigel. I say don't tempt fate."

Andrew lowered his voice. "She does have an impish side underneath all that ethereal serenity."

As plates grew lighter and dishes were cleared from the tables, Mist, Maisie, and Betty all helped serve pecan pie, adding champagne ice cream for those who wanted it. And, as it was every Christmas Eve at the Timberton Hotel, both stomachs and hearts were full by the end of the meal.

Chapter Sixteen

With Betty, Clive and others—Sally and Marge among them—insisting on cleaning up after dinner, Mist—after a fair amount of nudging her out of the kitchen—left them to the task and joined guests in the front parlor. She collected Rain from Michael, who had taken his favorite place by the fire. Holding the sweet baby close, she looked around the room and wondered if everything seemed brighter this year or if she was imagining it. Had her perception of life changed? She'd always loved the Christmas season, finding it filled with joy. But this year the tree seemed a little more festive, the fire a bit warmer, the music richer. In fact, she'd felt this for months, ever since... was that it? She looked down, knowing the answer lay with the little human in her arms. Nothing had been the same since Rain entered the world. The world with Rain was not the same as the world without Rain. Her existence changed everything, and Mist was grateful for such a precious gift.

"Gather round, all ye would-be carolers!" Wes took a seat on the piano bench and let his fingers race across the keys playfully. "We are taking requests tonight, fine folks. What shall it be?"

"How about 'The First Noel'?" Clara suggested. She moved closer to the piano, and Wes began to play. Andrew followed as did others until most of the guests surrounded the piano and began to sing. The carols continued with "Joy to the World," "O Come All Ye Faithful," and "Deck the Halls."

Of course, in view of the angel theme this year, "Hark the Herald Angels Sing" was a must.

"First written as a poem in 1739!" the professor announced with glee, which earned him the following good-natured ribbing from Clive.

"Nigel, absolutely no one needed to know that!"

That brought a wave of laughter all around.

"He's kidding, of course," Betty said in Clive's defense.

"We know." Clara laughed. "We all love the professor's tidbits of knowledge."

An attempt at singing "The Twelve Days of Christmas" together as a group resulted in even more hearty laughter as the proper order of words and verses became challenging.

At Wes's suggestion once the room quieted down, Elisa offered a solo of "O Holy Night" so exquisite that it left several with misty eyes.

"Oh my!" Betty exclaimed. "What an amazing voice!"

"I heard Wes say earlier that she's opera trained," Giulia said. "She's magnificent. And we know opera well in Florence."

Clive put another log on the fire and then led Betty to the Christmas tree. As he did each year, he lifted an ornament from a branch at the back of the tree where he'd hidden it that afternoon. The silver sparkled as he brought into the light and handed it to Betty.

"Oh, Clive! An angel! It's lovely!" Betty took the ornament from him and let it sway from her fingertips. As with all the ornaments he'd given her over the years, it featured a tiny Yogo sapphire—in this case, two, one on each angel wing. "It's a perfect addition to the others you've made. And so appropriate for this year."

"And I have something else to give out, if Mist and Michael will do me the honor of stepping toward the tree." He lifted another ornament from behind the tree, this one covered in tissue paper and ribbon to hide the design.

Mist approached from beneath the archway to the lobby, and Michael rose from his chair by the fireplace. Both stood before the tree eagerly, each a little curious at the other's enthusiasm.

"I have a rather special commission here," Clive said.

Betty leaned toward Clara and whispered. "This should be interesting!"

"Oh? How intriguing," Clara whispered back. "And you have the inside scoop."

"I do," Betty said, watching Mist and Michael stand before Clive, both excited and somewhat confused. "And it's very sweet. Just watch what happens next."

"One of you asked for this to be designed for the other." Clive let the ornament dangle. "So go ahead and take it."

Both Mist and Michael reached forward to take the ornament simultaneously, stopping when they realized what they were doing. They looked at each other with surprise, then at Clive for an explanation.

"That's right," Clive said. "You each asked me to make the same thing. The *exact* same thing."

"Really?" Michael's eyebrows lifted.

"So this is why we couldn't take it ahead of time," Mist said.

"You didn't really need to polish it up 'just a bit more' like you said." Michael looked at Mist. "He gave you the same excuse?"

Mist nodded. "Very clever, Clive."

"Thank you," Clive said, proud of himself for pulling this off. "Because if either of you took it early, the other would wonder why I couldn't bring it out if you came by."

"So open it!" Kylie said.

"Well," Michael said. "We do know what it looks like."

"That's true," Mist agreed.

"But we don't!" Kylie extended her arms to the side and looked around the room as if presenting her case.

"She has a point," the professor said. "Let's see what all these covert shenanigans were about."

As others around the room echoed the same sentiments, Mist—at Michael's insistence—removed the tissue paper from the ornament and held it out for everyone to see.

"It's an angel just like the one you got," Kylie said, pointing to Betty's ornament.

"Yes and no," Clive said. "This one is engraved for a special little angel for her first Christmas."

"Oh, how lovely!" Giulia exclaimed, looking closer. "Rain's First Christmas." Giulia and Tom exchanged glances.

"Clive, we may need to get your email," Tom said. "Do you ship to Italy?"

"Of course." Clive beamed with pride.

Wes slid onto the piano bench. "I think this calls for a song." He began to play "Angels We Have Heard on High," and others joined in, singing.

"This is for you, sweet girl," Mist said, looking down at Rain snuggled up against her. She held the ornament in front of Rain, who reached out to grab it. "We'll put it on the tree here and take it home later."

"And speaking of home," Michael said. "Should I take our

little angel home now? I imagine you have a bit of artwork ahead of you tonight."

"Yes, that's an excellent idea." Mist and Michael carefully transferred Rain between them. Michael said a few good-nights all around and then left. And Mist, after checking that beverages and treats were plentiful, did the same, leaving the happy crowd to share the rest of the evening together. As always on Christmas Eve, she had a project to finish.

MIST SAT BACK and looked at the small canvases before her. She loved the tradition of giving mini paintings to the guests each year to take home with them. This not only gave them something to remember their visit by, but it served as a thank-you for what Mist considered to be a gift *from* them: the joy of their presence at the hotel. Because that's how she—and Betty and Clive—saw the guest visits. They received as much from those who visited as the guests received themselves. People brought with them their stories of locations far and wide. They offered insight into life outside of Timberton, and they shared their talents, the musical joy from Elise and Wes this year being a perfect example.

It might seem to others that Mist always knew what she would paint for each guest, but it was far from the truth. She preferred to observe how a guest's visit went, what conversations took place, what personal insight each person allowed. Each guest was unique, and each visit was unique. This held true with repeat guests as well as well as new ones. Life flowed according to its own design, and it was often unpredictable. And so, the images she ended up with usually came to her at the last minute.

Looking at the miniature paintings now, she hoped each

one would have meaning for its recipient even if it only reflected a bit of humor or a random memory.

Taking squares of fabric that she'd cut to a perfect size, she folded the fabric around each painting and tied a satin ribbon around each. After which she slid them between branches of the tree in the front parlor and headed home.

Chapter Seventeen

CHRISTMAS MORNING WAS ALWAYS A JOYFUL TIME AT THE Timberton Hotel in spite of the knowledge that guests would soon be parting ways and heading off in different directions. The few days spent together seemed to have a magical effect on those spending that time at the hotel. Somehow, even with all their differences, they came together as friends, as family. What it was that made this happen could not be defined, but it was as real as the angel ornaments that now flew off to others. As real at the tree of wishes from the year before. As real as a gingerbread house that had been built yet another year. Whatever magic made this happen, it was undeniable.

Breakfast the day after the extravagant meal the night before was often light, but this year, Clive and Duffy and even Wild Bill—with very specific directions from everyone—decided to put on a country breakfast fitting the Montana mountain area the town of Timberton was in. Banning the women from the kitchen—though not with those exact words—the three of them whipped up a feast of scrambled eggs, slabs of ham, bacon, country fried potatoes, and biscuits and gravy.

In one concession to accepting help, Mist was allowed to make the biscuits from scratch, using the excuse that Kylie wanted to help with the baking. But both Mist and the young baker were politely urged out of the kitchen once the biscuits were in the oven. Whether they saw the two of them sneak homemade huckleberry jam onto the buffet and place a bowl of fresh salsa by the eggs, no one knew. However, no one doubted the source of the cup of apple puree that appeared at the professor's place.

Elisa and Wes were the first to arrive, followed within minutes by Kylie, who had waited at the bottom of the stairs for Scarlet to descend. Both were in a noticeably more cheerful mood than when they first arrived, even demonstrating some curious conspiratorial whispering as they took a seat together. Mist watched the two of them from the juice bar and smiled, grateful for the joy they had found during their stay.

Giulia and Tom soon joined the others, as did Clara and Andrew, the professor, and Michael. As Christmas morning breakfast was reserved for hotel guests only, townsfolk spent the morning at home with their own families and friends. Sally was an exception to this, seeing as Wild Bill was present in a very limited and closely monitored role—-with much teasing involved—in the kitchen.

Their appetites satisfied yet again after the Christmas Eve feast the night before, the crowd moved into the front parlor where gifts had appeared under the tree overnight. Kylie was thrilled to see that Elisa and Wes had managed to bring presents with them. Clara and Andrew had agreed not to exchange gifts, saying whatever trip they decided to take in the coming year would be their gift to each other.

Betty came into the room to refill the bowl of glazed cinnamon nuts, and Clive joined her after helping with kitchen clean-up. Hollister also took a seat where he could enjoy watching the morning festivities. Bacon curled up on the floor next to him.

"We have a tradition here at the Timberton Hotel," Mist said once all the guests' gifts had been exchanged. "We're so grateful for the time you've spent with us, for the gift of sharing your lives with us. In appreciation of that, we'd like to give you something to take home with you, to remember your holiday here."

Mist reached into the tree and pulled the packages out that she'd hidden the night before. One by one, she passed them around the room to the new guests, and one by one, the satin ribbons and fabric fell to the side as the gifts were unwrapped.

"This is beautiful!" Giulia exclaimed as she held up the miniature painting of a gold angel holding a sweet baby blanket with a rocking horse on it. "Thank you so much!"

Elisa and Wes were next to show their painting. "How clever," Elise said. "An angel holding a ribbon of musical notes."

And Kylie laughed with delight at her painting of an angel holding a rolling pin.

"That's so she can look after you in the kitchen," Mist said. "I suspect you'll be spending a lot of time there over the years."

Kylie nodded.

Scarlet was the last to hold her painting up, which she did with tears in her eyes. Yet they were happy tears. The painting of an angel holding a dog with a halo was something she would always treasure.

"Because sometimes we can have joy within sadness," Mist said. "And I think I see a little more joy coming up the walkway." She looked out the window and looked back at Scarlet, smiling. "You called Addison, didn't you?"

Scarlet smiled and nodded. "Yes. You made me realize it was okay to open my heart."

Kylie jumped up. "I already knew it. She told me last night!"

"Well, aren't you the secret keeper!" Elisa exclaimed. "You didn't say a word! No wonder you two were acting so mysterious at breakfast."

Kylie and Scarlet both went to the front door, and the other guests heard bits and pieces of conversation in the lobby. When Scarlet returned, the sweet dog that had come to her the day before was at her side. Addison and Kylie stood a few feet behind.

"This is Lily, everyone," Scarlet said. "She and I will be starting a new adventure together." A spontaneous round of applause followed. Scarlet looked down at Lily, and Lily looked up at her. It was obvious to everyone that this was a match meant to be.

"And you drove here, right?" Clara asked.

"Yes, from just outside Spokane." Scarlet laid her hand on Lily's head.

"Oh good. So it won't be too hard to get her home." Clara smiled and added, "To her *new* home."

"It'll be our first road trip together," Scarlet said.

"She does love car rides," Addison said. "Wait until you see how quickly she jumps in the car."

"Then it'll be one of many road trips."

"Speaking of trips," Betty said to Clara and Andrew, "where do you think you might go this year?"

Clara hunched her shoulders and held her hands out to each side, palms up. "I have no idea." She looked at Andrew. "Do you?"

"Maybe Alaska?" Andrew suggested. "Or Portugal? Or somewhere closer, like New Orleans or Charleston?"

"Or London," the professor suggested. "I'll be taking a trip there this year to visit family. I could show you around if the timing is right."

"Oh, there's an idea!" Clara said. She looked at Andrew, who agreed, and then back at the professor. "Let's talk more about that later."

"Brilliant," the professor replied.

"I vote on a trip right now," Tom said, standing up. "Outside to enjoy the beautiful day. *Andiamo!*"

"*Andiamo!*" the others repeated as they stood, even Kylie, who then turned to Giulia and whispered, "What does that mean?"

"Let's go," Giulia whispered back.

Kylie pointed toward the front door. "*Andiamo! Buon Natale!*"

Chapter Eighteen

Mist, Maisie, and Betty stood on the front porch of the hotel, watching the activity in the front yard. Rain and Cora snuggled against their mothers, each comfortably held in organic cotton wraps with a holly stencil print that Mist had designed for the sweet girls' first Christmas. Matching caps completed the outfits. Michael had made a point of taking photos earlier, knowing they would cherish these days for years to come.

A steady snowfall overnight had left a blanket of soft powder on the ground, just the right amount for frolicking around under what was now a blue sky on a sunny day. If there was such a thing as winter combined with summer, this day was it.

"It's a doggone nice Christmas afternoon," Clive said as he stepped onto the porch. All three women groaned as he nodded toward Scarlet and Hollister, who were coordinating an enthusiastic game of fetch. Lily and Bacon were having a blast chasing balls and bringing them back.

"You had to say it, didn't you?" Betty chuckled.

"I really did," Clive said, looking quite proud of himself. "Someone had to. Didn't even *paws* to say it."

Betty tapped his shoulder playfully. "Enough!"

"Okay, okay." Clive laughed as he moved over next to Mist and Maisie. "And how are these two real live angels enjoying their first Christmas?" Clive tickled Rain's tummy through the fabric wrap and then did the same to Cora. Both babies responded with gurgling giggles.

"Cora has loved having family here," Maisie said. "They've showered her with attention. Clayton's parents absolutely spoil her. And Clay Jr. has so much fun showing off as the big brother. I think she might grow into being the life of the party. She's comfortable in social settings."

Mist looked down at Rain and smiled. "This one's pretty easygoing. She enjoys peaceful times the best, I think, like when Michael is reading to her or when we listen to soft music. But she's comfortable in the kitchen too. Pots and pans don't seem to bother her when they clatter a bit."

"Well, that's a good thing!" Clive exclaimed, rubbing his stomach.

Mist looked across to the corner of the yard where Elise, Wes, and Kylie were busy building a snowman. After getting the snowman's head built, Kylie ran up to the porch.

"I think all we need now is a carrot for his nose."

"A carrot for a nose? Hmm." Mist tapped her own nose. "I think we can make that happen." She retreated into the hotel and returned with two carrots, one larger than the other. "Here you go. See which one is a better fit."

Kylie turned to run to the snowman but then turned back. "Thanks, Mist. *Buon Natale!*"

"You're welcome, Kylie. *Buon Natale* to you too. Oh, and…" Mist leaned forward and whispered. "Are you glad you got out of the car?"

"Yes! I am." Kylie skipped over to the snowman, a carrot in each hand. She held each potential nose up, made a decision, and gave the snowman his finishing touch.

"Clara and Andrew went out for a walk, didn't they?" Clive asked, directing his question at no one in particular.

"Yes," Betty said. "And Giulia and Tom went for a drive to see some of the Montana countryside before they move on tomorrow. Michael and the professor went with them as tour guides of sorts."

"Are they going back to Italy straightaway?" Maisie asked as she rocked Cora in her arms.

"Not for another week, I believe," Mist said. "They're going to visit California first. San Francisco, I believe, and then a drive along the coast. And I think New York after that." She had been pleased to hear that they'd see more of the country before leaving.

Shrieks of laughter erupted from the corner of the yard as Kylie and her parents switched from building the snowman to a snowball fight. Mist smiled as she watched Kylie smack her father with a perfect pitch. He reciprocated with an equally accurate but gentler toss.

"I'd better get back to Clay and the family." Maisie said a quick goodbye and Merry Christmas and left for her home. Clive followed, setting off to stock the wood by the fireplace and tend to some "odds and ends" around the hotel—his term for tinkering on miscellaneous tasks.

Left together on the porch, Mist and Betty looked at the activity in the yard—dogs chasing balls, their humans laughing with delight, the family engaged in a snowball war—and then turned to each other.

"I think you did it again, Mist," Betty said. "It's another beautiful Christmas."

"*We* did," Mist replied. "We all help make the holidays

special. You run this lovely hotel, Clive keeps the fireplace glowing and warm—"

"—and provides quality control for baked goods…" Betty added.

"Yes." Mist laughed. "He's quite dependable for that."

"And Maisie is wonderful about helping in the kitchen and with the flowers," Betty said. "Even with Cora now, she's always lending a hand."

"You see? It's everyone." Mist kissed the top of Rain's head and lowered her voice to a whisper. "Everyone, sweet girl, that's how it happens, that's how we come together." She nodded toward the yard and turned her attention back to Betty. "It's the guests and what they bring with them. It's a type of magic that we have here in Timberton."

"And it happens every year," Betty said with wonder. "It's amazing."

"Yes, it is."

"And next year?"

Mist smiled, knowing Betty already knew the answer. But she answered anyway, just to hear the words. "Next year? More of the same, of course."

Betty's Cookie Exchange Recipes

Betty's Cookie Exchange Recipes

Glazed Cinnamon Nuts
Snowball Cookies
Frosted Gingerbread Cookies
Josie's Fudge
Crème Brûlée Cookies
Easy Christmas Bark
Orange Crisps
Gingerbread Sandwich Cookies
The Best Old Fashioned Molasses Sugar Cookies
Crackle Double Chocolate Cookies
Walnut Butter Cookies
Glazed Fruitcake Cookies
Dutch Letter Almond Bars
Red Velvet Cupcakes
Sour Cream Sugar Cookies
Rolo Cookie Bars
Sparkling Angel Cookies (from Kim)
Pecan Kisses
Old-Fashioned Sugar Cookies
Iced Peppermint Candy Cookies

GLAZED CINNAMON NUTS
(a family recipe)

Ingredients:
- 1 cup sugar
- 1/4 cup water
- 1/8 teaspoon cream of tartar
- Heaping teaspoon of cinnamon
- 1 tablespoon butter
- 1-1/2 cups walnut halves

Directions:

Boil sugar, water, cream of tartar, and cinnamon to soft boil stage (236°).

Remove from heat. Add butter and walnuts.

Stir until walnuts separate. Place on waxed paper to cool.

SNOWBALL COOKIES
(Submitted by Shelia Hall)

Ingredients:
- 1 cup unsalted butter softened
- 5 tablespoons granulated sugar
- 2 teaspoons pure vanilla extract
- 1/4 teaspoon fine-grain sea salt
- 2 cups all-purpose flour
- 2 cups finely chopped walnuts, almonds or pecans
- 1 1/2 cups confectioners sugar

Directions:

Blend softened butter with powdered sugar. Add vanilla.

Mix in salt, flour, and chopped pecans.

Form dough into 1-inch balls or flattened cookies and place on an ungreased cookie sheet.

Bake in a 325 degree oven for 20 minutes. Roll in powdered sugar while hot. Let cool and roll again in powdered sugar.

FROSTED GINGERBREAD COOKIES
(Submitted by Petrenia Etheridge)

Ingredients:
- 1/2 cup butter
- 1/2 cup brown sugar, packed
- 1/2 cup molasses
- 1 teaspoon salt
- 2 teaspoons cinnamon
- 2 teaspoons ginger
- 1 teaspoon vanilla
- 1 egg
- 2-3 cups self rising flour

Frosting:
- 1-2 cups powdered sugar
- 1 teaspoon vanilla
- 2 tablespoons milk

Directions:

In a saucepan, melt butter and stir in sugar, salt, and molasses. Add in cinnamon and ginger and stir well.

Remove from heat and add vanilla and egg and stir well.

Slowly pour into 2 cups flour and mix. Add in extra flour as needed for rolled cookies.

Roll into a ball and cover with plastic wrap and chill for 1-2 hrs.

Roll out onto floured surface about 1/4 inch thick and use gingerbread man cookie cutter or round biscuit cutter.

Bake at 350 for 8-10 minutes. Frost when completely cool.

Josie's Fudge
(Submitted by Catherine Ann Tremble)

Ingredients:
- 3 cups of sugar
- 2/3 cups of evaporated milk
- 1 1/2 sticks of butter
- 1 package chocolate chips
- 1 jar marshmallow cream
- 1 teaspoon vanilla

Directions:

Put sugar, evaporated milk, and butter in medium size pan and cook over medium high heat, stirring constantly until a rolling boil. Cook for 5 minutes.

Remove from heat, and add one package of chocolate chips. Stir until mixed well.

Add a jar of marshmallow cream. Mix well. Add vanilla extract. Stir well.

Drop by tablespoons onto foil to create "fudge drops."

Option: Pour half of the mixture into a bread pan. Top with coconut/condensed milk mixture, then top that with the rest of the fudge to make a "mounds" fudge.

Crème Brûlée Cookies
(Submitted by Petrenia Etheridge)

Ingredients:
- 1/2 cup butter, softened
- 1/2 cup oil
- 1/2 cup sugar
- 1/2 cup powdered sugar
- 1 large egg
- 2 teaspoon vanilla
- 2 cups all purpose flour
- 1/2 teaspoon baking soda
- 1/2 teaspoon salt

Frosting
- Block of cream cheese, softened
- 6 tablespoons butter, softened
- 2 1/2 cups powdered sugar
- 1/2 teaspoon granulated sugar per cookie

Directions:

Mix butter, oil, and sugars and beat on high for about 4 minutes.

Add egg and vanilla and beat until combined.

Mix dry ingredients and add to mixture at low speed until combined.

Use ice-cream scoop or spoon and scoop about 2 tbsp dough and form into balls and flatten halfway on a cookie sheet with parchment paper. Cover and chill for 2-3 hrs.

Bake at 350 for 8 minutes. Let cool on cookie sheet.

For frosting, mix butter and cream cheese until fluffy. Add powdered sugar. Spread on cookies and sprinkle granulated sugar on top. Option: Use a torch to brûlée the tops.

Easy Christmas Bark
(Submitted by Lanette Fields)

Ingredients:
- 10-12 oz package of butterscotch chips
- 10-12 oz package of white chocolate chips
- 10-12 oz package of milk chocolate chips
- 10-12 oz package of dark chocolate chips
- 10-12 oz package of semisweet chocolate chips
- 9.5-10 oz package of mini milk chocolate M&Ms
- 16 oz can of cocktail peanuts (use 1/2 can or to taste)

Directions:

Line 2 large baking sheets including sides with parchment paper. Set aside.

Add all baking chips together in a microwave-safe bowl and heat 3 minutes at a time. Stir melted mixture until smooth.

Add half a can of peanuts and all M&Ms and stir until well mixed.

Quickly pour mixture evenly onto each baking sheet and smooth out.

Chill in refrigerator until set.

Break into pieces. If too hard to break apart, set out for 30 minutes.

Serve immediately or store in freezer-safe container for up to 3 months.

ORANGE CRISPS
(Submitted by Brenda Ellis)

Ingredients:
- 1 cup shortening
- 1 teaspoon grated orange peel
- 1/2 cup sugar
- 2 1/2 cups flour
- 1/2 cup brown sugar
- 1/4 teaspoon salt
- 1 tablespoon orange juice
- 1/4 teaspoon baking soda
- 1 egg

Directions:

Cream shortening. Add sugar and orange juice and cream well. Add egg and orange peel.

Sift flour, salt, and soda together, adding a little at a time to the shortening mixture.

Place by teaspoon full on an ungreased cookie sheet.

Bake at 375 for 10 to 12 minutes.

Yields 7 dozen small cookies.

Option: Can substitute lemon in place of orange.

Gingerbread Sandwich Cookies
(Submitted by Cecile VanTyne)

Ingredients:
　Cookie Ingredients:
　2 cups of all-purpose flour
　2 teaspoon ground cinnamon
　1/2 teaspoon ground ginger
　½ teaspoon nutmeg
　½ teaspoon salt
　1/4 teaspoon ground cloves
　3/4 teaspoon baking soda
　3/4 cup packed light brown sugar
　8 tablespoons unsalted butter, melted
　1/4 cup molasses
　3 tablespoons crystallized ginger, finally chopped (no substitution)
　1 large egg
　1/4 cup buttermilk
　1 teaspoon vanilla extract

Cream Cheese Filling:
　6 tablespoons unsalted butter, room temperature
　1 1/2 cups powdered sugar
　6 oz cream cheese cut into 6-8 pieces, softened
　1/2 teaspoon vanilla extract
　Pinch of salt

Garnish
　Powdered sugar for dusting

Directions:

Whisk flour, cinnamon, ground ginger, nutmeg, salt, cloves, and baking soda together in a medium bowl. Set aside.

Whisk brown sugar, melted butter, molasses, and crystallized ginger in a separate large bowl until combined. Whisk in egg, buttermilk and vanilla until combined. Add flour mixture and stir with a rubber spatula just until the dough comes together. Cover bowl with plastic wrap and refrigerate for at least 1 hour up to 24.

Preheat oven to 350 degrees. Line two baking sheets with parchment paper or a nonstick mat. Roll dough into balls using one scant tablespoon. Space balls evenly about 2 inches apart. Bake cookies one sheet at a time, until puffed and just set about 11-13 minutes. Let cookies cool on sheet for 5 minutes then transfer to wire rack to cool completely before frosting.

Using a stand mixer fitted w/paddle attachment, beat butter and powdered sugar on med-high speed until fluffy, about 2 minutes. With mixer running, add cream cheese 1 piece at a time and continue to beat until smooth, about 30 seconds. Beat in vanilla extract and a pinch of salt as needed.

Spoon or pipe 1 tablespoon of frosting evenly onto the bottom of 24 cookies. Top with remaining 24 cookies, bottom sides down. (If the frosting is very soft, refrigerate for 15 minutes before filling.) Then dust with powdered sugar.

Store cookies in an airtight container in the fridge. Bring to room temp before serving. Enjoy!

THE BEST OLD-FASHIONED MOLASSES SUGAR COOKIES
(Submitted by Alma Collins)

Ingredients:
- 1-1/2 cups butter, softened
- 2 cups granulated sugar
- ½ cup dark molasses
- 2 eggs, beaten
- 4 teaspoons baking soda
- 4 cups all-purpose flour
- 1 teaspoon ground cloves (I used allspice)
- 1 teaspoon ground ginger
- 2 teaspoons ground cinnamon
- 1 teaspoon salt
- Turbinado or sparkling sugar to coat the unbaked cookies

Directions:

In a medium bowl, beat the sugar and butter until light and fluffy. Stir in the eggs and molasses until completely blended.

In a separate large bowl, mix all the remaining dry ingredients together.

Add the butter mixture to the flour mixture and mix until combined completely.

Cover the dough tightly and refrigerate overnight.

IMPORTANT: The dough needs to be thoroughly chilled. Allow at least 4-6 hours to chill. When the dough is ready to be rolled, it will be very stiff.

Preheat the oven to 350°.

Roll the dough into 1-inch balls and coat them with the Turbinado sugar.

Bake the cookies on a sheet pan, placed 1-2 inches apart, for 10-12 minutes. The cookies should crackle on top and have golden edges. Recipe makes 6-8 dozen, depending on size.

CRACKLE DOUBLE CHOCOLATE COOKIES
(Submitted by Patti Rusk)

Ingredients:
- 1 box of chocolate cake mix
- 1 1/2 cups chocolate chips
- 1 8oz tub Cool Whip
- 1 egg
- 1 1/2 cups powdered sugar
- Spray oil for cookie scoop or hands

Directions:

Using whisk, mix cake mix (dry from box), egg, and Cool Whip until well blended. Stir in chocolate chips.

Using sprayed cookie scoop or sprayed hands, form into 1-inch round balls. Roll in powdered sugar.

Bake at 350 degrees for 12-15 minutes. Cool completely in wire rack.

Store in airtight container.

Walnut Butter Cookies
(Submitted by Patti Rusk)

Ingredients:
   1 cup salted butter, softened
   2 cups powder sugar
   1 3/4 cups all-purpose flour
   1 cup chopped walnuts
   1 teaspoon vanilla extract

Directions:

In a large mixing bowl, combine butter and 1 cup powder sugar. With electric mixer, beat at medium speed until light and creamy.

Add flour, walnuts, and vanilla extract, continue beating until blended.

Divide dough in half and roll each half into an 8-inch log. Wrap logs in plastic wrap and refrigerate overnight.

Slice logs into 1/2-inch slices. Placing 2 inches apart on parchment-lined baking sheet. Freeze for 15 minutes.

Bake at 350 degrees for 12 minutes until edges of cookies are golden brown. Cool completely on wire rack.

In shallow dish, dredge cookies with remaining 1 cup of powder sugar.

Serve immediately or store in airtight container separated by wax paper.

GLAZED FRUITCAKE COOKIES
(Submitted by Patti Rusk)

Ingredients:
- 1 1/4 cups spiced rum
- 1/2 cup finely chopped candied red cherries
- 1/2 cup finely chopped candied green cherries
- 1/2 cup finely chopped dried pineapple
- 1/2 cup finely chopped crystallized ginger
- 1/2 cup finely chopped candied orange
- 1 cup unsalted butter, softened (not melted)
- 1 3/4 cups sugar divided
- 1/4 cup light brown sugar firmly packed
- 2 large eggs, room temperature
- 1 teaspoon rum extract
- 3 1/2 cups all purpose flour
- 1 teaspoon baking soda
- 1 teaspoon salt
- 1 teaspoon nutmeg
- 1 teaspoon ground cinnamon
- 1 teaspoon round ginger
- 1/2 teaspoon ground cloves
- 1 cup chopped toasted pecans

Directions:

In medium microwave-safe bowl, combined rum, cherries, pineapple, crystallized ginger, and orange, microwave on high until hot 2-3 minutes. Let stand at room temperature for at least one hour stirring occasionally. Drain fruit mixture. Set aside.

Preheat oven to 350°F.

Using a stand mixer fitted with a paddle, beat the butter, 1 1/4 cups of gradated sugar and brown sugar at medium speed until fluffy, 2-3 minutes, occasionally scrape the size of the bowl. The eggs, one at a time beating well after each addition. Beat in rum extract.

In a medium bowl, whisk together flour, baking soda, salt, nutmeg, cinnamon, ground ginger, and cloves. Add flour mixture to butter mixture all at once. Beat at low speed just until combined stopping to scrape sides of bowl. Fold in the fruit mixture and pecans. Dough will be sticky.

On a rimmed plate, place remaining 1/2 cup of granulated sugar. Using a 2 tbsp cookie scoop, scoop dough and shape into balls. Roll in sugar and place 1 1/2-2 inches apart on baking sheets lined with parchment paper. Using the palm of your hand, gently flatten the balls into 1-inch thickness.

Bake until light gold brown and cookies are set around edges about 12 minutes. Let cool for three minutes on baking sheets and let cool completely on wire racks.

Place Rum Drizzle in a pastry bag and drizzle onto cooled cookies.

Rum Drizzle
    1 cup powder sugar
    1 1/2 tablespoons heavy whipping cream
    1 tablespoon spiced rum
    2 teaspoon unsalted butter melted
    1/4 teaspoon salt

In medium bowl stir together all ingredients until smooth. Use immediately.

DUTCH LETTER ALMOND BARS

When you can't get to Pella, Iowa, or the Netherlands!
(Submitted by Vera Kenyon)

Ingredients:
- 1 cup butter, melted
- 1 - 7 or 8 oz package of almond paste
- 2 eggs plus 1 egg yolk, (save the egg white)
- 1 1/2 cups sugar
- 2 cups flour- white or almond
- 2 teaspoons of almond extract
- 1/2 teaspoon vanilla
- Sliced almonds
- Coarse sugar- like Turbinado or a colored sugar

Directions:

Preheat the oven to 325 degrees.

In mixer, combine ingredients and blend well.

Spread into a 9x13 or 10x15 inch pan. Brush with whipped egg white.

Sprinkle with sliced almonds and sugar.

Bake for 25-30 minutes until golden brown. Be careful not to overbake.

Betty's Cookie Exchange Recipes

Red Velvet Cupcakes
(Submitted by Alisha Collins)

Ingredients:
- 2 1/2 cups flour
- 1/2 cup unsweetened cocoa powder
- 1 teaspoon baking soda
- 1/2 teaspoon salt
- 2 cups sugar
- 1 cup (2 sticks) butter, at room temperature
- 4 eggs at room temperature
- 1 cup sour cream
- 1/2 cup buttermilk
- 1 bottle (1 ounce) red food coloring
- 2 teaspoons vanilla extract

Directions:

Preheat oven to 350 degrees and line 30 cupcake cups.

In a separate bowl, whisk together the flour, cocoa, baking soda, and salt. Set aside.

Cream together the butter and sugar together on medium speed until light and fluffy. This usually takes about 5 minutes.

Beat in eggs one at a time until fully incorporated, scraping bowl down between each egg.

Mix in sour cream, buttermilk, food coloring, and vanilla.

Gradually mix in flour mixture until just combined. Don't overmix!

Spoon batter into muffin cups until 2/3 full.

Bake 20-25 minutes until toothpick comes out clean.

Cool in pans for 5 minutes and then turn out onto wire racks to cool completely.

Tips:
 *If you don't have buttermilk, you can mix 1 tablespoon of vinegar or lemon juice to enough sweet milk (regular milk) to make 1 cup. Mix together and allow to set 5 minutes before using in recipe. If you only need 1/2 cup cut measurements in half.
 *Adjust cooking time by 10-15 minutes if making a multiple layer cake instead of cupcakes.
 *For a deeper chocolate flavor, use a dark cocoa and add 1 tablespoon more than what the recipe calls for.

Frosting:
 Vanilla Cream Cheese Frosting

 1 8 ounce package of cream cheese, softened
 1/4 cup (1/2 stick) butter, softened
 2 tablespoons sour cream
 2 teaspoons vanilla
 1 16 ounce package confectioner's sugar (10X), approximately 3 1/2 cups

 Cream together the cream cheese, butter, sour cream, and vanilla on medium speed until light and fluffy (approximately 3-4 minutes).
 Gradually blend in the powdered sugar until smooth and spreadable.
 Spread on cupcakes or your layer cake and enjoy.

Sour Cream Sugar Cookies
(Submitted by Betty Rufledt)

Ingredients:
- 2 cups sugar
- 3 eggs
- 1 cup sour cream
- 1 teaspoon soda
- 1 1/4 cups shortening
- 2 teaspoons vanilla
- 1 teaspoon baking powder
- 5 cups flour

Directions:

Cream sugar, shortening and eggs until fluffy. Add vanilla and sour cream.

Gradually add dry ingredients.

Refrigerate for 1 1/2 hrs. Roll 1/4 of dough.

Roll out 1/2 inch for thick cookies or thinner if desired.

Cut into shapes and sprinkle with sugar and place on greased cookie sheet.

Bake at 375 for 10 minutes until set.

Betty's Cookie Exchange Recipes

ROLO COOKIE BARS (GLUTEN-FREE VERSION)
(Submitted by Colleen Galster)

Ingredients:
- 3/4 cup butter
- 3/4 cup brown sugar
- 1 teaspoon vanilla extract
- 1 large egg
- 1 egg yolk
- 1 3/4 cups gluten free flour
- 1/2 teaspoon baking soda
- 1/4 teaspoon salt
- 1 cup chocolate chips
- 1 1/2 cups Rolo candies

Directions:

Preheat oven to 350 degrees. Grease and line an 8-inch square pan with parchment paper making sure the 2 sides overhang.

In a large mixing bowl cream butter and brown sugar until pale and creamy. Add vanilla, egg and the egg yolk and beat with mixer until combined.

Add flour, baking soda and salt and beat until a soft dough forms.

Add chocolate chips and mix well. Divide the dough in half and press the first half into the bottom of the pan to form an even layer. Scatter Rolo candies all over the dough.

Take the other half of the dough and break it into pieces and place it on top of the Rolos. Gently spread it out so most of the Rolos are covered.

Cook for approximately 18-20 minutes or until golden brown. Leave to cool completely in the pan. Cut into bars and enjoy!

SPARKLING ANGEL COOKIES
(Submitted by Kim Davis of Cinnamon and Sugar and a Little Bit of Murder)

Using a boxed cake mix for the base, these light, chewy cookies are a breeze to make.
  Makes 3 dozen

Ingredients:
  1 box Angel Food cake mix
  1 egg
  1/3 cup water
  1/2 teaspoon orange extract
  Coarse sparkling sugar, or your color choice of sanding sugar.

Directions:
  Line a baking sheet with parchment paper. This is a must as the cookies are sticky!
  Add the cake mix to a large bowl. Whisk the egg, water, and extract together, then stir into the cake mix until smooth. Dough will be loose. Chill for 1 hour.
  Preheat the oven to 350 degrees (F).
  Using a tablespoon-sized cookie scoop, drop spoonfuls of dough onto the prepared baking sheet. Space them at least 2 to 3 inches apart since these cookies spread.
  Generously sprinkle the tops of the unbaked cookies with sparkling sugar (or your choice of sanding sugar).
  Bake for 9 to 10 minutes until edges are a light golden color. Remove from oven and cool cookies on the baking sheet for 10 minutes, then transfer to a wire rack to cool completely.
  Store leftovers in an airtight container with parchment or wax paper between the layers.

PECAN KISSES
(Submitted by Petrenia Etheridge)

Ingredients:
- 1 egg white, beaten stiff
- 1/2 cup brown sugar
- 1 teaspoon vanilla
- 2- 2 1/2 cups pecan halves

Directions:

Mix together stiff egg white, sugar and vanilla.

Dip pecan halves in mixture to cover completely and place individually on a greased baking sheet or parchment paper about 2 inches apart.

Bake at 200 for 30 minutes, turn oven off and leave pecans in for another 30 minutes. Take out and place in candy dish.

OLD-FASHIONED SUGAR COOKIES
Recipe from the 1800s
(Submitted by Betty Escobar)

Ingredients:
- 1 cup (two sticks) butter, softened
- 1 cup sugar
- 2 eggs, beaten well
- 1 tablespoon milk
- 2 teaspoons vanilla
- 2-3 cups flour
- 1 teaspoon baking powder

Directions:

Cream butter and sugar together. Sift baking powder with flour.

Add milk, well beaten eggs, and vanilla.

Add enough flour to roll out. Cut into desired shapes with cookie cutters.

Bake at 375 degrees for ten minutes.

Tip: This is a typical Victorian recipe, which was simply a list of ingredients and essentially no instructions. Recommend starting with 2 cups of flour and then adding more as needed to get the dough to a consistency where you are able to pinch the dough together and form a ball.

Betty's Cookie Exchange Recipes

ICED PEPPERMINT CANDY COOKIES
(Submitted by Molly Elliott)

Ingredients:
- 1/2 cup butter (one stick), softened
- 1/3 cup white sugar
- 1 large egg, beaten
- 1 1/2 cups all-purpose flour
- 1/8 teaspoon salt
- 2 tablespoons water
- 1 teaspoon vanilla
- 1/4 cup crushed peppermint candy canes
- Option: Use toffee bits instead of crushed candy canes

Icing:
- 1/3 cup confectioners' sugar
- 3 teaspoons warm water
- 1 tablespoon crushed peppermint candy canes, or to taste

Directions:

Cream butter and sugar together. Add egg.

Add flour and salt. Mix all ingredients together.

Add crushed candy canes and form combine to form a soft dough.

Roll into balls the size of a small walnut and place 1 inch apart on greased cookie sheets.

Bake at 350 degrees for 10-12 minutes. Let cool a few minutes on cookie sheet before moving to a wire rack.

Icing:

Mix powdered sugar and water together until smooth.

Dip cooled cookies into the icing and then sprinkle with crushed candy canes. Let set before serving.

Recipe Notes

Recipe Notes

Recipe Notes

Recipe Notes

Acknowledgments

The expression "it takes a village" applies to many things, and writing a book is certainly one of them. *Angels at Moonglow* only exists because of Annie Sarac's top-notch editing, which always makes a story shine, Elizabeth Christy's rope of developmental support when I fell into plot holes and needed help to climb out, Paul Sterrett's unwavering emotional support, and the efforts of many others who helped with various tasks along the way. The beautiful cover is thanks to the artistic talents of Mariah Sinclair. I'm also grateful to the Georgetown Writers for their constant encouragement.

As with other books in the Moonglow Christmas Series, Betty's cookie exchange gathers not only fictional treats but also recipes from readers. This year, thanks for these go to Kim Davis and her blog, Cinnamon and Sugar and a Little Bit of Murder, Petrenia Etheridge, Shelia Hall, Lanette Fields, Betty Escobar, Colleen Galster, Catherine Ann Tremble, Patti Rusk, Cecile VanTyne, Alma Collins, Brenda Ellis, Vera Kenyon, Alisha Collins, and Betty Rufledt. What are you waiting for? Grab your kitchen apron and let's get baking!

Books by Deborah Garner

The Paige MacKenzie Series

Above the Bridge

When NY reporter Paige MacKenzie arrives in Jackson Hole, it's not long before her instincts tell her there's more than a basic story to be found in the popular, northwestern Wyoming mountain area. A chance encounter with attractive cowboy Jake Norris soon has Paige chasing a legend of buried treasure passed down through generations. Sidestepping a few shady characters who are also searching for the same hidden reward, she will have to decide who is trustworthy and who is not.

The Moonglow Café

The discovery of an old diary inside the wall of the historic hotel soon sends NY reporter Paige MacKenzie into the underworld of art and deception. Each of the town's residents holds a key to untangling more than one long-buried secret, from the hippie chick owner of a new age café to the mute homeless man in the town park. As the worlds of western art and sapphire mining collide, Paige finds herself juggling research, romance, and danger.

Three Silver Doves

The New Mexico resort of Agua Encantada seems a perfect destination for reporter Paige MacKenzie to combine work with well-deserved rest and relaxation. But when suspicious jewelry shows up on another guest, and the town's storyteller goes missing, Paige's R&R is soon redefined as restlessness and risk. Will an unexpected overnight trip to Tierra Roja Casino lead her to the answers she seeks, or are darker secrets lurking along the way?

Hutchins Creek Cache

When a mysterious 1920s coin is discovered behind the Hutchins Creek Railroad Museum in Colorado, Paige MacKenzie starts digging into four generations of Hutchins family history, with a little help from the Denver Mint. As legends of steam engines and coin mintage mingle, will Paige discover the true origin of the coin, or will she find herself riding the rails dangerously close to more than one long-hidden town secret?

Crazy Fox Ranch

As Paige MacKenzie returns to Jackson Hole, she has only two things on her mind: enjoy life with Wyoming's breathtaking Grand Tetons as the backdrop and spend more time with handsome cowboy Jake Norris as he prepares to open his guest ranch. But when a stranger's odd behavior leads her to research Western filming in the area—in particular, the movie *Shane*, will it simply lead to a freelance article for the *Manhattan Post*, or will it lead to a dangerous, hidden secret?

Sweet Sierra Gulch

Paige MacKenzie isn't convinced there's anything "sweet" about Sweet Sierra Gulch when she arrives in the small California Gold Rush town. Still, there's plenty of history as well as anticipated romance with her favorite cowboy, Jake Norris. But when the owner of the local café goes missing, Paige is determined to find out why. Will she uncover a dangerous secret in the town's old mining tunnels, or will curiosity land her in over her head?

The Sadie Kramer Flair Series

A Flair for Chardonnay

When flamboyant senior sleuth Sadie Kramer learns the owner of her favorite chocolate shop is in trouble, she heads for the California wine country with a tote-bagged Yorkie and a slew of questions. The fourth generation Tremiato Winery promises answers, but not before a dead body turns up at the vintners' scheduled Harvest Festival. As Sadie juggles truffles, tips, and turmoil, she'll need to sort the grapes from the wrath in order to find the identity of the killer.

A Flair for Drama

When a former schoolmate invites Sadie Kramer to a theatre production, she jumps at the excuse to visit the Monterey Bay area for a weekend. Plenty of action is expected on stage, but when the show's leading lady turns up dead, Sadie finds herself faced with more than one drama to follow. With both cast members and production crew as potential suspects, will Sadie and her sidekick Yorkie, Coco, be able to solve the case?

A Flair for Beignets

With fabulous music, exquisite cuisine, and rich culture, how could a week in New Orleans be anything less than fantastic for Sadie Kramer and her sidekick Yorkie, Coco? And it is... until a customer at a popular patisserie drops dead face-first in a raspberry-almond tart.

A competitive bakery, a newly formed friendship, and even her hotel's luxurious accommodations offer possible suspects. As Sadie sorts through a gumbo of interconnected characters, will she discover who the killer is, or will the killer discover her first?

A Flair for Truffles

Sadie Kramer's friendly offer to deliver three boxes of gourmet Valentine's Day truffles for her neighbor's chocolate shop backfires when she arrives to find the intended recipient deceased. Even more intriguing is the fact that the elegant heart-shaped gifts were ordered by three different men. With the help of one detective and the hindrance of another, Sadie will search San Francisco for clues. But will she find out "whodunit" before the killer finds a way to stop her?

A Flair for Flip-Flops

When the body of a heartthrob celebrity washes up on the beach outside Sadie Kramer's luxury hotel suite, her fun in the sun soon turns into sleuthing with the stars. The resort's wine and appetizer gatherings, suspicious guest behavior, and casual strolls along the beach boardwalk may provide clues, but will they be enough to discover who the killer is, or will mystery and mayhem leave a Hollywood scandal unsolved?

A Flair for Goblins

When Sadie Kramer agrees to help decorate for San Francisco's high-society Halloween shindig, she expects to find whimsical ghosts, skeletons, and jack-o-lanterns when she shows up at the Wainwright Mansion—not a body. With two detectives, a paranormal investigator turned television star, and a cauldron full of family members cackling around her, Sadie and her sidekick Yorkie are determined to find out who the killer is. Will an old superstition help lead to the truth? Or will this simply become one more tale in the mansion's haunted history?

A Flair for Shamrocks

When flamboyant senior sleuth Sadie Kramer's car breaks down outside a small Oregon beach town, the repair lands her in unexpected lodging above an Irish pub for St. Patrick's Day. With pub games, green beer, and a potbellied pig named Paddy in the mix, it's bound to be a unique holiday. But not all is what it seems in Irishton, especially when the owner of the pub turns up dead. An assortment of local characters could be guilty, but only one is the killer. Sadie and her sidekick Yorkie will need the luck of the Irish to solve the mystery.

The Moonglow Christmas Series

Mistletoe at Moonglow

The small town of Timberton, Montana, hasn't been the same since resident chef and artist, Mist, arrived, bringing a unique new age flavor to the old western town. When guests check in for the holidays, they bring along worries, fears, and broken hearts, unaware that Mist has a way of working magic in people's lives. One thing is certain: no matter how cold winter's grip is on each guest, no one leaves Timberton without a warmer heart.

Silver Bells at Moonglow

Christmas brings an eclectic gathering of visitors and locals to the Timberton Hotel each year, guaranteeing an eventful season. Add in a hint of romance, and there's more than snow in the air around the small Montana town. When the last note of Christmas carols has faded away, the soft whisper of silver bells from the front door's wreath will usher guests and townsfolk back into the world with hope for the coming year.

Gingerbread at Moonglow

The Timberton Hotel boasts an ambiance of near-magical proportions during the Christmas season. As the aromas of ginger, cinnamon, nutmeg, and molasses mix with heartfelt camaraderie and sweet romance, holiday guests share reflections on family, friendship, and life. Will decorating the outside of a gingerbread house prove easier than deciding what goes inside?

Nutcracker Sweets at Moonglow

When a nearby theater burns down just before Christmas, cast members of *The Nutcracker* arrive at the Timberton Hotel with only a sliver of holiday joy. Camaraderie, compassion, and shared inspiration combine to help at least one hidden dream come true. As with every Christmas season, this year's guests will face the New Year with a renewed sense of hope.

Snowfall at Moonglow

As holiday guests arrive at the Timberton Hotel with hopes of a white Christmas, unseasonably warm weather hints at a less-than-wintery wonderland. But whether the snow falls or not, one thing is certain: with resident artist and chef, Mist, around, there's bound to be a little magic. No one ever leaves Timberton without renewed hope for the future.

Yuletide at Moonglow

When a Yuletide festival promises jovial crowds, resident artist and chef, Mist, knows she'll have her hands full. Between the legendary Christmas Eve dinner at the Timberton Hotel and this season's festival events, the unique magic of Christmas in this small Montana town offers joy, peace, and community to guests and townsfolk alike. As always, no one will return home without a renewed sense of hope for the future.

Starlight at Moonglow

As the Christmas holiday approaches, a blizzard threatens the peaceful ambiance that the Timberton Hotel usually offers its guests. Even resident artist and chef, Mist, known to work near miracles, has no control over the howling winds and heavy snowfall. But there's always a bit of magic in this small Montana town, and this year's storm may just find it's no match for heartfelt camaraderie, joyful inspiration, and sweet romance.

Joy at Moonglow

Each holiday season is unique in the small Montana town of Timberton. New and returning guests bring their dreams, cares, and worries, and always leave with lighter hearts and renewed hope for the future. But no season has ever been as special as this one. Because, to everyone's delight, wedding bells will be ringing. Thanks to the heartfelt efforts of many and no shortage of sweet romance, this year will be the most joyful of all

Evergreen Wishes at Moonglow

Christmas in the small town of Timberton, Montana, is always filled with holiday traditions, exquisite cuisine, and heartfelt camaraderie.

When a majestic evergreen tree is placed in the center of town, inviting ornaments containing wishes, townsfolk and visitors are soon pondering what their hopes and dreams might be. Although wishes can't always come true, some just might with a bit of holiday magic.

Angels at Moonglow

The small Montana town of Timberton always provides a joyful Christmas retreat for visitors as well as those who live in the area.

This year, an angel ornament project offers guests and local townsfolk a chance to reflect on others in their lives. As always, time spent together, exquisite food, and camaraderie allow guests a chance to trade worries for a sense of peace and hope for the future.

Additional Titles:

Cranberry Bluff

Molly Elliott's quiet life is disrupted when routine errands land her in the middle of a bank robbery. Accused and cleared of the crime, she flees both media attention and mysterious, threatening notes to run a bed-and-breakfast on the Northern California coast. Her new beginning is peaceful until five guests show up at the inn, each with a hidden agenda. As true motives become apparent, will Molly's past come back to haunt her, or will she finally be able to leave it behind?

Sweet Treats: Recipes from the Moonglow Christmas Series

Delicious recipes, including Glazed Cinnamon Nuts, Cherry Pecan Holiday Cookies, Chocolate Peppermint Bark, Cranberry Drop Cookies, White Christmas Fudge, Molasses Sugar Cookies, Lemon Crinkles, Spiced Apple Cookies, Swedish Coconut Cookies, Double-Chocolate Walnut Brownies, Blueberry Oatmeal Cookies, Cocoa Kisses, Angel Crisp Cookies, Gingerbread Eggnog Trifle, Dutch Sour Cream Cookies, and more!

More Sweet Treats: Recipes from the Moonglow Christmas Series

Chocolate Crinkle Cookies, Amish Sugar Cookies, Yuletide Coconut Cherry Cookies, Almond Crunch Bars, Chai Tea Shortbread Cookies, Peanut Butter Chocolate Fudge, Peppermint Snowball Cookies, Cranberry Walnut Pinwheels, Gingerbread Kiss Cookies, Eggnog Cookies with Rum Butter Icing, Glazed Fruitcake Cookies, Dutch Letter Almond Bars, Crème Brûlée Cookies, Caramel Apple Cookies, Date Nut Torte Squares, Salted Peanut Cookies, Chocolate Waffle Cookies, and more!

For more information on Deborah Garner's books:

Facebook: https://www.facebook.com/deborahgarnerauthor

Twitter: https://twitter.com/PaigeandJake

Website: http://deborahgarner.com

Mailing list: http://eepurl.com/bj-clD

Milton Keynes UK
Ingram Content Group UK Ltd.
UKHW032046201124
451474UK00005B/435